My Sweet Orange Tree

The story of a little boy who discovered pain

José Mauro de Vasconcelos

translated by Alison Entrekin

CANDLEWICK PRESS

Original text copyright © 1968 by Editora Melhoramentos Ltda, Brazil
English translation copyright © 2019 by Alison Entrekin

Published by arrangement with Pushkin Press

MINISTÉRIO DA CULTURA
Fundação BIBLIOTECA NACIONAL

Work originally published by Pushkin Press with the support of
the Brazilian Ministry of Culture/National Library Foundation
Obra publicada com o apoio do Ministério da Cultura do Brasil/
Fundação Biblioteca Nacional

Library of Congress Catalog Card Number 2018960536
ISBN 978-1-5362-0328-8

19 20 21 22 23 24 LSC 10 9 8 7 6 5 4 3 2 1

Printed in Crawfordsville, IN, U.S.A.

This book was typeset in Granjon.

Candlewick Press
99 Dover Street
Somerville, Massachusetts 02144

visit us at www.candlewick.com

For

Mercedes Cruañes Rinaldi
Erich Gemeinder
Francisco Marins
as well as
Helene Rudge Miller (Birdie!)
Nor can I forget
my "son"
Fernando Seplinsky

* * *

For those who have never died

Ciccillo Matarazzo
Arnaldo Magalhães de Giacomo

* * *

In loving memory of my brother Luís (King Luís)
and my sister Glória. Luís gave up on life at the age of
twenty, and Glória, at twenty-four, didn't
think life was worth living either.

Equally as precious is my memory of Manuel Valadares,
who taught me the meaning of tenderness at the age of six.

May they all rest in peace!
and now
Dorival Lourenço da Silva
(Dodô, neither sadness nor nostalgia kill!)

CONTENTS

·PART ONE·
At Christmas, Sometimes the Devil Child Is Born

·PART TWO·
When the Baby Jesus Appeared in All His Sadness

PART ONE

At Christmas, Sometimes the Devil Child Is Born

CHAPTER ONE

The Discoverer of Things

We were strolling down the street hand in hand, in no hurry at all. Totoca was teaching me about life. And that made me really happy, my big brother holding my hand and teaching me things. But teaching me things out in the world. Because at home I learned by discovering things on my own and doing things on my own; I'd make mistakes, and because I made mistakes, I always ended up getting beaten. Until not long before that, no one had ever hit me. But then they heard things and started saying I was the devil, a demon, a sandy-haired sprite. I didn't want to know about it. If I wasn't outside, I'd have started to sing. Singing was pretty. Totoca knew how to do something besides sing: he could whistle. But no matter how hard I tried to copy him, nothing came out. He cheered me up by saying it was normal, that I didn't have a whistler's mouth yet. But because I couldn't sing on the outside, I sang on the inside. It was weird at first, but then it felt really nice. And I was remembering a song Mama used to sing when I was really little. She'd be standing at the washtub, with a cloth tied about her head to keep the sun off it. With an apron around her waist, she'd spend hours and hours plunging her hands into the water, turning soap into lots of suds. Then she'd wring out the clothes and take them to the clothesline, where she'd peg them all out and hoist it up high. She did the same thing with all the clothes. She washed clothes from Dr. Faulhaber's house to help with the household expenses. Mama was tall and thin, but very beautiful. She was brown from the sun, and her hair was straight and black.

When she didn't tie it up, it hung down to her waist. But the most beautiful thing was when she sang, and I'd hang around, learning.

"Sailor, sailor
Sailor of sorrow
Because of you
I'll die tomorrow . . .

The waves crashed
Dashed on sand
Off he went
My sailor man . . .

A sailor's love
Lasts not a day
His ship weighs anchor
And sails away . . .

The waves crashed . . ."

That song had always filled me with a sadness I couldn't understand.

Totoca gave me a tug. I came to my senses.

"What's up, Zezé?"

"Nothing. I was singing."

"Singing?"

"Yeah."

"Then I must be going deaf."

Didn't he know you could sing on the inside? I kept quiet. If he didn't know, I wasn't going to teach him.

We had come to the edge of the Rio–São Paulo Highway. On it, there was everything. Trucks, cars, carts, and bicycles.

"Look, Zezé, this is important. First we take a good look one way, and then the other. Now go."

We ran across the highway.

"Were you scared?"

I was, but I shook my head.

"Let's do it again together. Then I want to see if you've learned."

We ran back.

"Now you go. No balking, 'cause you're a big kid now."

My heart beat faster.

"Now. Go."

I raced across, almost without breathing. I waited a bit, and he gave me the signal to return.

"You did really well for the first time. But you forgot something. You have to look both ways to see if any cars are coming. I won't always be here to give you the signal. We'll practice some more on the way home. But let's go now, 'cause I want to show you something."

He took my hand, and off we went again, slowly. I couldn't stop thinking about a conversation I'd had.

"Totoca."

"What?"

"Can you feel the age of reason?"

"What's this nonsense?"

"Uncle Edmundo said it. He said I was 'precocious' and that soon I'd reach the age of reason. But I don't feel any different."

"Uncle Edmundo is a fool. He's always putting things in that head of yours."

"He isn't a fool. He's wise. And when I grow up, I want to be wise and a poet and wear a bow tie. One day I'm going to have my picture taken in a bow tie."

"Why a bow tie?"

"Because you can't be a poet without a bow tie. When Uncle Edmundo shows me pictures of poets in the magazine, they're all wearing bow ties."

"Zezé, you have to stop believing everything he tells you. Uncle Edmundo's a bit cuckoo. He lies a bit."

"Is he a son of a bitch?"

"You've already been slapped across the mouth for using so many swear words! Uncle Edmundo isn't that. I said 'cuckoo.' A bit crazy."

"You said he was a liar."

"They're two completely different things."

"No, they're not. The other day, Papa was talking about Labonne with Severino, the one who plays cards with him, and he said, 'That old son of a bitch is a goddamn liar.' And no one slapped him across the mouth."

"It's OK for grown-ups to say things like that."

Neither of us spoke for a moment.

"Uncle Edmundo isn't . . . What does 'cuckoo' mean again, Totoca?"

He pointed his finger at his head and twisted it around.

"No, he isn't. He's really nice. He teaches me things, and he only smacked me once and it wasn't hard."

Totoca started.

"He smacked you? When?"

"When I was really naughty and Glória sent me to Gran's house. He wanted to read the newspaper, but he couldn't find his glasses. He searched high and low, and he was really mad. He asked Gran where they were, but she had no idea. The two of them turned the house upside down. Then I said I knew where they were and if he gave me some money to buy marbles, I'd tell him. He went to his waistcoat and took out some money.

"'Go get them and I'll give it to you.'

"I went to the clothes hamper and got them. And he said, 'It was you, you little rascal!' He gave me a smack on the backside and put the money away."

Totoca laughed.

"You go there to avoid getting smacked at home

and you get smacked there. Let's go a bit faster or we'll never get there."

I was still thinking about Uncle Edmundo.

"Totoca, are children retired?"

"What?"

"Uncle Edmundo doesn't do anything, and he gets money. He doesn't work, and City Hall pays him every month."

"So what?"

"Well, children don't do anything. They eat, sleep, and get money from their parents."

"Retired is different, Zezé. A retired person has already worked for a long time, their hair's turned white, and they walk slowly like Uncle Edmundo. But let's stop thinking about difficult things. If you want to learn things from him, fine. But not with me. Act like the other boys. You can even swear, but stop filling your head with difficult things. Otherwise I won't go out with you again."

I sulked a bit and didn't want to talk anymore. I didn't feel like singing either. The little bird that sang inside me had flown away.

We stopped and Totoca pointed at the house.

"There it is. Like it?"

It was an ordinary house. White with blue windows. All closed up and quiet.

"Yeah. But why do we have to move here?"

"It's good to stay on the move."

We stood gazing through the fence at a mango tree on one side and a tamarind tree on the other.

"You're such a busybody, but you have no idea what's going on at home. Papa's out of a job, isn't he? It's been six months since he had the fight with Mr. Scottfield and they kicked him out. Did you know Lalá's working at the factory now? And Mama's going to work in the city, at the English Mill? Well, there you go, silly. It's all to save up to pay the rent on this new house. Papa's a good eight months behind on the other one. You're too young to have to worry about such sad things. But I'm going to have to help out at mass, to pitch in at home."

He stood there awhile in silence.

"Totoca, are they going to bring the black panther and the two lionesses here?"

"Of course. And old slave-boy here is going to have to take apart the chicken coop."

He gave me a kind of sweet, pitiful look.

"I'm the one who's going to take down the zoo and reassemble it here."

I was relieved. Because otherwise I'd have to come up with something new to play with my littlest brother, Luís.

"So, you see how I'm your friend, Zezé? Now, it wouldn't hurt for you to tell me how you did 'it' . . ."

"I swear, Totoca, I don't know. I really don't."

"You're lying. You studied with someone."

"I didn't study anything. No one taught me. Unless it was the devil who taught me in my sleep. Jandira says he's my godfather."

Totoca was puzzled. He even rapped me across the head a few times to try to get me to tell him. But I didn't know how I'd done it.

"No one learns that kind of thing on their own."

But he was at a loss for words because no one had actually seen anyone teach me anything. It was a mystery.

I remembered what had happened a week earlier. It had left the family in a flap. It had started at Gran's house, when I sat next to Uncle Edmundo, who was reading the newspaper.

"Uncle."

"What is it, son?"

He moved his glasses to the tip of his nose, as all grown-ups do when they get old.

"When did you learn to read?"

"At around six or seven years of age."

"Can five-year-olds learn to read?"

"I suppose so. But no one likes to teach them because it's really too young."

"How did you learn to read?"

"Like everyone else, with first readers. Going 'B plus A makes BA.'"

"Does everyone have to learn like that?"

"As far as I know, they do."

"Absolutely everyone?"

He looked at me, intrigued.

"Look, Zezé, that's how everyone learns. Now, let me finish reading. Go look for guavas in the backyard."

He pushed his glasses back up his nose and tried to concentrate on reading. But I didn't leave.

"What a shame!"

It was such a heartfelt exclamation that he moved his glasses back down his nose.

"I'll be darned. You're persistent, aren't you?"

"It's just that I walked all the way over here just to tell you something, sir."

"OK, then, tell me."

"No. Not like that. First I need to know when your next pension day is."

"Day after tomorrow," he said with a little smile, studying me.

"And what day is after tomorrow?"

"Friday."

"Well, on Friday could you bring me a Silver King from the city?"

"Slow down, Zezé. What's a Silver King?"

"It's the little white horse I saw at the cinema. Its owner is Fred Thomson. It's a trained horse."

"You want me to bring you a little horse on wheels?"

"No, sir. I want the sort with a wooden head and reins. That you stick a tail on and run around. I need to practice because later I'm going to work in films."

He laughed.

"I see. And if I do, what's in it for me?"

"I'll do something for you, sir."

"You'll give me a kiss?"

"I'm not big on kisses."

"A hug?"

I looked at Uncle Edmundo and felt really sorry for him. The little bird inside me said something. And I remembered what I'd heard people say so many times, that Uncle Edmundo was separated from his wife and had five children. But he lived all on his own and walked so slowly. . . . Maybe he walked slowly because he missed his children. And his children never came to visit him.

I walked around the table and hugged him tight. I felt his white hair brush my forehead. It was really soft.

"This isn't for the horse. What I'm going to do is something else. I'm going to read."

"Come again, Zezé? You can read? Who taught you?"

"No one."

"You're lying."

I backed away, and from the doorway I said, "Bring me my horse on Friday and you'll see if I can read or not!"

Later, when it was nighttime and Jandira lit the lantern since the power company had cut off the electricity because the bill hadn't been paid, I stood on my tiptoes to see the "star." It was a picture of a star on a piece of paper with a prayer underneath it to protect the house.

"Jandira, can you pick me up? I'm going to read that."

"Enough with the tall tales, Zezé. I'm busy."

"Pick me up and I'll show you."

"Look, Zezé, if you're up to something, you'll be in trouble."

She picked me up and took me behind the door.

"Go on, then, read. This I want to see."

Then I read, for real. I read the prayer that asked the heavens to bless and protect the house and to ward off evil spirits.

Jandira put me down. Her mouth was open.

"Zezé, you memorized that. You're tricking me."

"I swear, Jandira. I can read everything."

"No one reads without having learned to. Was it Uncle Edmundo? Gran?"

"No one."

She went to fetch a page from the newspaper, and I read it without any mistakes. She gave a little shriek and called Glória. Glória became nervous and went to get Alaíde. In ten minutes, a crowd of neighbors had gathered to see the phenomenon.

That was what Totoca wanted me to tell him.

"He taught you and promised you the horse if you learned."

"It's not true."

"I'm going to ask him."

"Go ahead. I don't know how to explain it, Totoca. If I did, I'd tell you."

"Then let's go. You'll see. When you need something . . ."

He grabbed my hand angrily and began to drag me home. Then he thought of something to get revenge.

"Serves you right! You learned too soon, silly. Now you'll have to start school in February."

·17·

It had been Jandira's idea. That way the house would be peaceful all morning long and I'd learn some manners.

"Let's practice crossing the highway again. Don't think that when you go to school, I'll be your nanny, taking you across all the time. If you're so clever, you can learn this too."

"Here's the horse. Now, let's see this."

He opened the newspaper and showed me a sentence in an ad for a medicine.

"In all good pharmacies and drugstores," I read.

Uncle Edmundo went to get Gran from the backyard.

"Mama, he even read 'pharmacies' correctly."

They both started giving me things to read, and I read everything.

Gran started muttering that all was lost.

Uncle Edmundo gave me the horse, and I hugged him again. Then he held my chin and, in a wavering voice, said, "You're going to go far, you little monkey. It's no accident your name's José. You'll be the sun, and the stars will shine around you."

I didn't get it and wondered if he really was a bit cuckoo.

"That's something you don't understand. It's the story of Joseph. I'll tell you when you're a bit bigger."

I was crazy about stories. The harder they were, the more I liked them.

I patted my little horse for a long time, and then I looked up at Uncle Edmundo and said, "Do you think I'll be a bit bigger by next week, Uncle?"

CHAPTER TWO

A Certain Sweet Orange Tree

In our family, each older sibling brought up a younger one. Jandira had taken care of Glória and another sister, who'd been given away to have a proper upbringing in the north. Totoca was Jandira's little darling. Then Lalá had taken care of me until not long ago. For as long as she liked me. Then I think she got sick of me or fell madly in love with her boyfriend, who was a dandy with baggy trousers and a short jacket just like the one in the song. When they used to take me for a "promenade" (that's what her boyfriend called a stroll) on Sundays, he'd buy me some really yummy sweets so I wouldn't tell anyone. I couldn't even ask Uncle Edmundo what "promenade" meant or the whole family would find out.

My other two siblings had died young, and I had only heard about them. They say they were two little Apinajé Indians, very dark, with straight black hair. That's why they were given Indian names. The girl was called Aracy and the boy Jurandyr.

Then came my little brother Luís. Glória was the one who looked after him the most, then me. He didn't even need looking after, because there wasn't a cuter, quieter, better-behaved boy in the world.

That's why when he spoke in that little voice of his without a single mistake, as I was heading out into the street, I changed my mind.

"Zezé, are you going to take me to the zoo? It doesn't look like it's going to rain today, does it?"

How adorable. He spoke so well. That boy was going to be someone; he was going to go far.

I looked at the beautiful day with the sky all blue and didn't have the courage to lie. Because sometimes, if I wasn't in the mood, I'd say, "You're out of your mind, Luís. Just look at the storm coming!"

This time I took his little hand, and we went out for our adventure in the backyard.

The backyard was divided into three games. One was the zoo. Another was Europe, which was over by Julio's neat little fence. Why Europe? Not even my little bird knew. We played Sugarloaf Mountain cable cars there. We'd take the box of buttons and put them all on a string. (Uncle Edmundo called it twine. I thought twine were pigs, but he explained that pigs were swine.) Then we'd tie one end to the fence and the other to Luís's fingertips. We'd push all the buttons up to the top and let them go slowly, one by one. Each cable car was full of people we knew. There was a really black one, which was Biriquinho's. It wasn't unusual to hear a voice coming from over the fence, "Are you damaging my fence, Zezé?"

"No, Dona Dimerinda. See for yourself, ma'am."

"Now, that's what I like to see. Playing nicely with your brother. Isn't it better like that?"

It might have been nice, but when my "god-father" the devil gave me a nudge, there was nothing better than getting up to mischief. . . .

"Are you going to give me a calendar for Christmas, like last year?"

"What did you do with the one I gave you?"

"You can go inside and see, Dona Dimerinda. It's above the bag of bread."

She laughed and promised she would. Her husband worked at Chico Franco's general store.

The other game was Luciano. At first Luís was really scared of him and would tug on my trousers, asking to leave. But Luciano was my friend. Whenever he saw me, he'd screech loudly. Glória wasn't happy about it either and said that bats were vampires that sucked children's blood.

"It's not true, Gló. Luciano isn't like that. He's my friend. He knows me."

"You and your critter mania, talking to things . . ."

It was hard work convincing Luís that Luciano wasn't a critter. To us, Luciano was a plane flying at the Campo dos Afonsos air base.

"Look, Luís."

And Luciano would fly happily around us as if he understood what we were saying. And he did.

"He's an airplane. He's doing . . ."

I'd stop. I had to get Uncle Edmundo to tell me that word again. I didn't know if it was "acorbatics," "acrobatics," or "arcobatics." One of those. But I couldn't teach my little brother the wrong word.

But now he wanted the zoo.

We got quite close to the old chicken coop. Inside it, the two fair-feathered hens were pecking at the ground, and the old black one was so tame that we could even scratch her head.

"First let's buy our tickets. Hold my hand, 'cause it's easy for children to get lost in this crowd. See how busy it gets on Sundays?"

Luís would look around, see people everywhere, and hold my hand tightly.

At the ticket office, I stuck my belly out and cleared my throat to sound important. I put my hand in my pocket and asked the woman, "Until what age is entry free?"

"Five."

"So just one adult then, please."

I took two orange-tree leaves as tickets and we went in.

"First, son, you're going to see how beautiful the birds are. Look, parrots, parakeets, and macaws of every color. Those ones over there with the colorful feathers are scarlet macaws."

His eyes bulged with delight.

We strolled about, looking at everything. We saw so many things that I even noticed Glória and Lalá behind everything else, sitting on the bench, peeling oranges. Lalá was eyeing me. . . . Could they have found out? If they had, that zoo visit was going to end with a big paddling on someone's rear. And that someone could only be me.

"What's next, Zezé? What are we going to see now?"

I cleared my throat again and resumed my posture.

"Let's go and see the monkeys. Uncle Edmundo calls them simians."

We bought a few bananas and threw them to the monkeys. We knew it wasn't allowed, but the guards had their hands too full with such a big crowd.

"Don't get too close or they'll throw banana peels at you, pip-squeak."

"I really want to see the lions."

"We can go in a minute."

I shot another look over to where the two other "simians" were eating oranges. I'd be able to hear what they were talking about from the lions' cage.

"Here we are."

I pointed at the two yellow African lionesses. Luís said he wanted to pat the black panther's head.

"Are you out of your mind, pip-squeak? The black panther is the most terrible animal in the zoo. She was brought here because she'd bitten off and eaten eighteen tamers' arms."

Luís looked scared and pulled back his arm in fright.

"Did she come from a circus?"

"Yes."

"Which circus, Zezé? You never told me that before."

I thought and thought. Who did I know who had a name for a circus?

"Ah! She came from the Rozemberg Circus."

"Isn't that a bakery?"

It was getting harder and harder to trick him. He was growing smart.

"That too. We should sit down and have our lunch. We've walked a lot."

We sat down and pretended to be eating. But my ears were pricked, listening to what my sisters were saying.

"We should learn from him, Lalá. Look how patient he is with Luís."

"Yes, but Luís doesn't do what he does. It's evil, not mischief."

"So he's got the devil in his blood, but he's so funny. No one on the street can stay angry at him, no matter what he gets up to. . . ."

"He's not passing me without getting a paddling. One day he'll learn."

I shot an arrow of pity into Glória's eyes. She always came to my rescue, and I always promised her I wouldn't do it again.

"Later. Not now. They're playing so quietly."

She already knew everything. She knew that

I'd gone through the ditch into Dona Celina's back-yard. I'd been fascinated by the clothesline swinging a bunch of arms and legs in the wind. Then the devil told me that I could make all those arms and legs come tumbling down at the same time. I agreed that it would be really funny. I found a piece of sharp glass in the ditch, climbed up the orange tree, and patiently cut the line.

I almost fell down with it. There was a cry and people came running.

"Help, the line snapped."

But a voice coming from I don't know where yelled even louder.

"It was Seu Paulo's kid, the little pest. I saw him climbing the orange tree with a piece of glass."

"Zezé?"

"What, Luís?"

"How do you know so much about zoos?"

"I've been to a lot of them."

It was a lie. Everything I knew, Uncle Edmundo had told me. He'd even promised to take me to the zoo one day. But he walked so slowly that by the time we arrived, it wouldn't even be there anymore. Totoca had been once with Papa.

"My favorite is the one on Rua Barão de Drummond, in Vila Isabel. Do you know who the Baron of Drummond was? Of course you don't. You're too young to know these things. The Baron must have been really chummy with God. Because he was the one who helped God invent the lottery game that they sell tickets for in the Misery and Hunger bar and the zoo. When you're older . . ."

My sisters were still there.

"When I'm older what?"

"Boy, do you ask a lot of questions. When you're old enough, I'll teach you the lottery animals and their numbers. Up to twenty. From twenty to twenty-five, I know there's a cow, a bull, a bear, a deer, and a tiger. I don't know what order they're in, but I'm going to learn so I don't teach you the wrong thing."

He was growing tired of the game.

"Zezé, sing 'The Little House' for me."

"Here at the zoo? There's too many people."

"No. We've left already."

"It's really long. I'll just sing the bit you like."

I knew it was the part about the cicadas. I filled my lungs.

"*I live in a house*
atop a hill
down which
an orchard spills.
A little house
where one can see
far far off
the sea."

I skipped a few verses.

"*Among strange palms*
cicadas sing psalms.
The sun sets
with golden sails.
In the garden,
a nightingale."

I stopped. My sisters were still sitting there, wait-ing for me. I had an idea: I'd sing until nightfall. I'd outlast them.

No such luck. I sang the whole song, repeated it, then I sang "For Your Fleeting Love" and even "Ramona." The two different versions of "Ramona" that I knew . . . but they didn't budge. Then I got desperate. Better to get it over and done with. I went over to Lalá.

"Go ahead, give it to me."

I turned around and offered her my bum, clenching my teeth because Lalá was heavy-handed with the slipper.

It was Mama's idea.

"Today we're all going to see the house."

Totoca took me to one side and told me in a whisper, "If you tell anyone we've already been there, you've got it coming."

But it hadn't even occurred to me.

A whole crowd of us set off down the street. Glória held my hand and had orders not to let me out of her sight for one minute. And I held Luís's hand.

"When do we have to move, Mama?" asked Glória.

"Two days after Christmas, we have to start packing our stuff," said Mama, somewhat sadly.

She sounded so tired. I felt really sorry for her. Mama had worked all her life. She'd been working since the age of six, when the factory was built. They would sit her on a table, and she'd have to clean and dry tools. She was so tiny that she'd wet herself on the table because she couldn't get down by herself. That's why she never went to school or learned to read and write. When she told me, I was so sad I promised that when I was a poet and wise, I'd read her my poems.

Signs of Christmas were appearing in the shops and stores. Father Christmas had been drawn on every pane of glass. People were already buying cards to avoid the rush closer to the time. I had a vague hope that this time the Baby Jesus would be born in my heart. At any rate, maybe I'd improve a bit when I reached the age of reason.

"This is it."

Everyone loved it. The house was a little smaller. With Totoca's help, Mama untwisted a piece of wire that was holding the gate shut, and there was a stampede. Glória let go of my hand and forgot that she was becoming a young lady. She raced over to the mango tree and flung her arms around it.

"The mango tree's mine. I got here first."

Totoca did the same with the tamarind tree.

Nothing was left for me. I looked at Glória, almost crying.

"What about me, Gló?"

"Run around the back. There must be more trees, silly."

I ran, but I found only long grass and a bunch of thorny old orange trees. Next to the ditch was a small sweet orange tree.

I was disappointed. They were all going through the house claiming bedrooms.

I tugged on Glória's skirt.

"There was nothing else."

"You don't know how to look properly. Just wait a minute. I'll find you a tree."

And soon she came with me. She examined the orange trees.

"Don't you like that one? It's a fine tree."

I didn't like this one, or that one, or any of them. They all had too many thorns.

"I prefer the sweet orange tree to those ugly things."

"Where?"

I took her to see it.

"But what a lovely little orange tree! It doesn't have a single thorn. It has so much personality that you can tell it's a sweet orange tree from far off. If I were your size, I wouldn't want anything else."

"But I want a big tree."

"Think about it, Zezé. This one's still young. It's going to grow big — you'll grow together. You'll understand each other like brothers. Have you seen that branch? It's the only one, it's true, but it looks a bit like a horse made just for you."

I was feeling really hard done by. It reminded me of the Scotch bottle with angels on it that we'd seen once. Lalá had said, "That one's me." Glória picked one for herself, and Totoca took one for himself.

But what about me? I ended up being the little head behind all the others, almost wingless. The fourth Scottish angel that wasn't even a whole angel . . . I was always last. When I grew up, I'd show them. I'd buy an Amazon rain forest, and all the trees that touched the sky would be mine. I'd buy a store with bottles covered in angels, and no one would even get a piece of wing.

Sulking, I sat on the ground and leaned my anger against the little orange tree. Glória walked away, smiling.

"That anger of yours won't last, Zezé. You'll see that I was right."

I scratched at the ground with a stick and was beginning to stop sniffling when I heard a voice coming from I don't know where, near my heart.

"I think your sister's right."

"Everyone's always right. I'm the one who never is."

"That's not true. If you'd just take a proper look at me, you'd see."

With a start, I scrambled up and stared at the little tree. It was strange because I always talked to everything, but I thought it was the little bird inside me that made everything talk back.

"But can you really talk?"

"Can't you hear me?"

And it gave a little chuckle. I almost screamed and ran away. But curiosity kept me there.

"How do you talk?"

"Trees talk with everything. With their leaves, their branches, their roots. Want to see? Place your ear here on my trunk, and you'll hear my heartbeat."

I hesitated a moment, but seeing its size, my fear dissipated. I pressed my ear to its trunk and heard a faraway *tick . . . tick . . .*

"See?"

"Tell me something. Does everyone know you can talk?"

"No. Just you."

"Really?"

"I swear. A fairy once told me that when a little boy just like you befriended me, I would talk and be very happy."

"And will you wait?"

"What?"

"Until I move. It'll take more than a week. You won't forget how to talk, will you?"

"Never. That is, only for you. Do you want to see what a smooth ride I am?"

"How can . . . ?"

"Sit on my branch."

I obeyed.

"Now, rock back and forth and close your eyes."

I did as I was told.

"What do you think? Have you ever had a better horse?"

"Never. It's lovely. I'm going to give my horse Silver King to my little brother. You'll really like him."

I climbed down, loving my little orange tree.

"Look, I'm going to do something. Whenever I can, even before we move, I'm going to come and chat with you. Now I have to go. They're already out the front, about to head off."

"But friends don't say good-bye like that."

"Psst! Here comes my sister."

Glória arrived just as I was hugging the tree.

"Good-bye, my friend. You're the most beautiful thing in the world!"

"Didn't I tell you?"

"You did. Now if you offered me the mango or the tamarind tree in exchange for mine, I wouldn't want it."

She stroked my hair tenderly.

"Zezé, Zezé . . ."

We left holding hands.

"Gló, your mango tree's a bit dumb, don't you think?"

"It's too early to tell, but it does seem that way."

"What about Totoca's tamarind tree?"

"It's a bit awkward, why?"

"I don't know if I should tell you. But one day I'm going to tell you about a miracle, Gló."

CHAPTER THREE

The Lean Fingers of Poverty

When I put the problem to Uncle Edmundo, he gave it some serious thought.

"So that's what you're worried about?"

"Yes, sir. I'm afraid that when we move, Luciano won't come with us."

"Do you think this bat really likes you?"

"Of course."

"From the bottom of his heart?"

"I'm sure of it."

"Then you can be certain he'll go. He might take a while to show up at the new place, but one day he'll find the way."

"I've already told him the street name and number."

"Well, that makes it even easier. If he can't go because he's got other commitments, he'll send a sibling, a cousin, a relative of some sort, and you'll never notice."

But I still wasn't convinced. What good was the street name and number if Luciano didn't know how to read? Maybe he'd go along asking the birds, the praying mantis, the butterflies.

"Don't worry, Zezé. Bats are very good at finding their bearings."

"At finding what, Uncle?"

He explained what bearings meant, and I was even more impressed by how much he knew.

With my problem solved, I went out to tell everyone what was in store for us: the move. Most grown-ups said cheerfully, "You're moving, Zezé? How lovely! How wonderful! What a relief!"

The only one who didn't bat an eyelid was Biriquinho.

"Good thing it's only a few streets over. You'll be nearby. What about that thing I told you about?"

"When is it?"

"Tomorrow at eight, at the door to the casino. Folks are saying the owner of the factory ordered a truckload of toys. You going?"

"Yep. I'm taking Luís. Do you think I'll get something too?"

"'Course. He's a runt like you. Why? You think you're too big?"

He came closer, and I felt that I was still really small. Smaller than I'd thought.

"Because if I'm going to get a present . . . But now I've got things to do. See you there."

I went home and hovered around Glória.

"What's up, Zezé?"

"It'd be so nice if you could take us to the casino tomorrow. There's a truck from the city stuffed full of toys."

"Oh, Zezé. I have a pile of things to do. I have

to iron, I have to help Jandira get things ready for the move, I have to keep an eye on the pots on the stove. . . ."

"A bunch of cadets from Realengo are going."

Besides collecting pictures of Rudolph Valentino, who she called Rudy, and pasting them into a notebook, she had a thing for cadets.

"You've got to be kidding me: cadets at eight o'clock in the morning? Pull the other leg! Run along and play, Zezé."

But I didn't go.

"You know, Gló, it's not for me. I promised Luís I'd take him. He's so little. All children his age can think about is Christmas."

"Zezé, I already told you I'm not going. And that's a fib: you're the one who wants to go. You've got your whole life to get Christmas presents."

"But what if I die? What if I die without getting a present this Christmas?"

"You're not going to die so soon, my little old man. You'll live twice as long as Uncle Edmundo or Seu Benedito. Now, enough of this. Go play."

But I still didn't go. I made sure she bumped

into me everywhere she turned. She'd go to the chest of drawers to get something, and she'd find me sitting on the rocking chair, begging her with my eyes. Begging with your eyes really got to her. She'd go to fetch water from the washtub, and I'd be sitting in the doorway, looking at her. She'd go to the bedroom to get the clothes to be washed, and I'd be sitting on the bed, chin in hands, looking. . . .

She couldn't take it.

"Enough, Zezé. I've already told you that no means no. For heaven's sake, don't try my patience. Go play."

But again I didn't go. That is, I thought I wasn't going. But she picked me up, carried me out the door, and dumped me in the backyard. Then she went back inside and closed the doors to the kitchen and the living room. I didn't give up. I sat outside every window she was going to pass, because now she was starting to dust and make the beds. She'd see me peeking at her and would shut the window. She ended up shutting up the whole house so she wouldn't see me.

"Meanie! Evil witch! I hope you never marry a

cadet! I hope you marry a private, the sort who can't even afford to have his boots polished."

When I saw that I was wasting my time, I headed for the street, fuming.

I ran into Nardinho playing. He was squatting, staring at something, oblivious to everything else. I went over. He had made a little wagon out of a matchbox and tied it to the biggest beetle I'd ever seen.

"Wow!"

"Big, isn't it?"

"Wanna swap?"

"Why?"

"If you want some trading cards . . ."

"How many?"

"Two."

"You're kidding. A beetle this big and you'll only give me two?"

"There're heaps of beetles like that in the ditch behind Uncle Edmundo's house."

"I'll do it for three."

"Three, but you don't get to pick."

"Nothing doing. I get to pick at least two."

"Fine."

I gave him one of Laura La Plante that I had several of. And he picked one of Hoot Gibson and another of Patsy Ruth Miller. I put the beetle in my pocket and went on my way.

"Quick, Luís. Glória's gone to buy bread, and Jandira's reading in the rocking chair."

We crept down the hallway to the bathroom. I went to help him pee.

"Make it a big one, 'cause we're not allowed to go in the street during the day."

Afterward, I splashed water from the washtub on his face. I did the same to mine, and we went back to the bedroom.

I dressed him without making any noise. I put his shoes on him. Goddamn socks! They just get in the way is all they do. I buttoned up his little blue suit and looked for a comb. But his hair wouldn't stay down. Something had to be done about it. I couldn't find anything anywhere. No brilliantine, no oil. I went into the kitchen and came back with a little lard on my fingertips. I rubbed it on my palm and took a whiff first.

"It doesn't smell at all."

Then I slapped it on Luís's hair and started combing. His head full of ringlets was beautiful. He looked like Saint John with a lamb on his back.

"Now, you stand over there, so you don't get all wrinkled. I'm going to get dressed."

As I pulled on my trousers and white shirt, I looked at my brother.

What a beautiful child he was! There was no one more beautiful in Bangu.

I pulled on my tennis shoes, which had to last until I went to school the next year. I kept looking at Luís.

All lovely and neat like that, he could have been mistaken for a slightly older Baby Jesus. I was sure he was going to get lots of presents. When they set eyes on him . . .

I shuddered. Glória had just come back and was putting the bread on the table. I could hear the paper bag rustling.

We went hand in hand and stood in front of her.

"Doesn't he look lovely, Gló? I dressed him myself."

Instead of getting angry, she leaned on the door and looked up. When she lowered her head, her eyes were full of tears.

"You look lovely too. Oh! Zezé!"

She knelt down and held my head against her chest.

"Good God! Why does life have to be so hard for some?"

She pulled herself together and started fixing our clothes.

"I told you I couldn't take you. I really can't, Zezé. I have too much to do. First let's have breakfast, while I think of something. Even if I wanted to, there isn't enough time for me to get ready. . . ."

She poured us our coffee and sliced the bread. She continued staring at us with a look of despair.

"So much effort for a couple of lousy toys. But I guess there are too many poor people for them to give away really good things."

She paused and then went on. "It might be your only chance. I'm not going to stop you from going. But, my God, you're too small. . . ."

"I'll get him there safely. I'll hold his hand the

whole time, Gló. We don't even need to cross the highway."

"Even so, it's dangerous."

"No, it isn't, and I'm good at finding my bearings."

She laughed through her sadness.

"Now, who taught you that?"

"Uncle Edmundo. He said Luciano's good at it, and if Luciano's smaller than me, then I'll be better . . ."

"I'll talk to Jandira."

"Why bother? She'll say yes. All Jandira does is read novels and think about her boyfriends. She doesn't care."

"Let's do this: finish your breakfast and we'll go to the gate. If we see someone we know who's heading that way, I'll ask them to go with you."

I didn't even want to eat any bread, so as not to waste time. We went to the gate.

Nothing passed except time. But that ended up passing too. Along came Seu Paixão, the mailman. He waved to Glória, took off his cap, and offered to accompany us.

Glória kissed Luís and kissed me. She asked with a teary smile, "What was that thing about a private and his boots?"

"It's not true. I didn't mean it. You're going to marry an airplane major with a bunch of stars on his shoulder."

"Why didn't you go with Totoca?"

"He said he wasn't going. And that he wasn't in the mood to go lugging 'baggage' around."

We set off. Seu Paixão told us to go on ahead and went along delivering letters to the houses. Then he would quicken his step and catch up with us. He did it over and over. When we reached the highway, he laughed and said, "Boys, I've got to speed up. You're making me fall behind in my work. Now, you go that way. It's not at all dangerous."

He hurried off with the bundle of letters and papers under his arm.

I thought angrily, *Coward! Abandoning two little children on the highway after promising Glória that he'd take us.*

I held Luís's little hand even tighter, and we kept walking. His tiredness was beginning to show.

His steps were growing shorter and shorter.

"C'mon, Luís. It's close now. There're lots of toys."

He'd walk a little faster and then would go slower again.

"Zezé, I'm tired."

"I'll carry you a ways, OK?"

He stretched out his arms, and I carried him a bit. Boy, was he heavy, a lead weight. When we reached Rua do Progresso, I was the one panting.

"Now you walk a bit more."

The church clock chimed eight o'clock.

"Oh dear! We were supposed to be there early, at seven-thirty. But it's OK — there are lots of people and plenty of toys to go around. A truckload."

"Zezé, my foot hurts."

I knelt down.

"I'm going to loosen your shoelaces a little, and it'll feel better."

We were going slower and slower. It felt like we'd never get to the market. We still had to pass the school and turn right on the street of the Bangu Casino. And the worst part was that time was flying on purpose.

We arrived, dead on our feet. There was no one there. It didn't even look like toys had been given out. But they had, because the street was littered with crumpled tissue paper. Torn scraps of colored paper were strewn across the sand.

My heart began to race.

We walked up to the casino and found Seu Coquinho closing the doors.

"Seu Coquinho, is it all over?" I said in a fluster.

"Yep, Zezé. You came too late. It was mayhem."

He closed one side of the door and smiled kindly.

"There's nothing left. Not even for my nieces and nephews."

He closed the other side of the door and stepped into the street.

"Next year, you need to come earlier, you sleepyheads!"

"It's OK."

It wasn't. I was so sad and disappointed that I'd rather have died than have that happen.

"Let's sit down over there. We need to rest a little."

"I'm thirsty, Zezé."

"When we pass the pastry shop, we can ask

Seu Rozemberg for a glass of water. That's it for us today."

It was only then that he understood the tragedy. He didn't even speak, just looked at me, his bottom lip jutting out and eyes brimming.

"Don't worry, Luís. You know my little horse, Silver King? I'm going to ask Totoca to change his pole and give it to you for Christmas."

He sniffled.

"No, don't do that. You're a king. Papa said he named you Luís because it was a king's name. And a king can't cry in the street, in front of other people."

I leaned his head against my chest and stroked his curly hair.

"When I grow up, I'm going to buy a beautiful car like Manuel Valadares's. Remember, the Portuguese man who passed us once at the train station when we went to wave at the Mangaratiba Express? Well, I'm going to buy a beautiful big car like that, full of presents just for you. . . . But don't cry, 'cause kings don't cry."

My chest exploded with sorrow.

"I swear I'm going to buy one. Even if I have to kill and steal . . ."

It wasn't the little bird inside me saying that. It must have been my heart.

It was the only way. Why didn't Jesus like me? He even liked the ox and the donkey in the manger. But not me. He was punishing me because I was the devil's godson. He was punishing me by not giving my brother a present. But that wasn't fair to Luís, because he was an angel. There couldn't have been an angel in heaven that was better than him. . . .

Cowardly tears began to roll down my face.

"Zezé, you're crying. . . ."

"It'll pass soon. Besides, I'm not a king like you. I'm good for nothing. A naughty boy, really naughty . . . That's all."

"Totoca, have you been back to the new house?"

"No. Have you?"

"I pop over there whenever I can."

"But why?"

"I want to see how Pinkie is."

"Who the heck is Pinkie?"

"He's my orange tree."

"You found a name that really suits him. You're good at finding things."

He laughed and continued whittling what was going to be Silver King's new body.

"And how is he?"

"He hasn't grown at all."

"Nor will he if you keep watching him. What do you think? Is this how you wanted the pole?"

"Yes. Totoca, how is it that you know how to do everything? You can make cages, chicken coops, nurseries, fences, gates . . ."

"That's because not everyone was born to be a poet in a bow tie. But if you really wanted to, you could learn."

"I don't think so. One needs to have the 'inclination' to do those things."

He paused for a moment and looked at me, half laughing, half disapproving of the new word Uncle Edmundo had probably taught me.

Gran had come over and was in the kitchen

making French toast soaked in wine for Christmas Eve supper. It was all there was.

I said to Totoca, "And some people don't even have this much. Uncle Edmundo gave us the money for the wine and to buy things for the fruit salad for lunch tomorrow."

Totoca was making the new pole for free because he'd heard about what had happened at Bangu Casino. At least Luís would get something. Something old and secondhand, but something very beautiful, which I liked a lot.

"Totoca?"

"What?"

"Do you think we're going to get nothing at all from Father Christmas?"

"I don't think so."

"Tell me the truth. Do you think I'm as naughty, as bad, as everyone says?"

"Not *bad* bad. It's just that you've got the devil in your blood."

"When Christmas comes, I really wish I didn't! I hope that before I die, at least once in my life, the

Baby Jesus will be born in my heart instead of the devil child."

"Maybe next year . . . Why don't you learn from me and do what I do?"

"What do you do?"

"I don't expect anything. That way I don't get disappointed. Jesus isn't as good as everyone says. 'Cause the priest says that even if the Catechism says . . ."

He paused, unsure if he should go on.

"Even if it says what?"

"Well, let's just say that you were really naughty and didn't deserve a thing. But what about Luís?"

"He's an angel."

"And Glória?"

"She is too."

"And me?"

"Well, sometimes you . . . you . . . use my things, but you're good."

"And Lalá?"

"She hits hard, but she's good. One day she's going to sew me a bow tie."

"And Jandira?"

"Jandira is Jandira, but she isn't bad."

"And Mama?"

"Mama's very good; she feels sorry for me when she smacks me, and she does it gently."

"And Papa?"

"Hmm! I'm not sure about him. He never gets lucky. I think he must have been like me, the bad one of the family."

"Well, then. Everyone in the family is good. So why isn't Jesus good to us? Now, go to Dr. Faulhaber's house and see the size of the table, piled high. The Villas-Boases' house, too. And Dr. Adaucto Luz's house — don't even get me started. . . ."

For the first time, I saw that Totoca was almost crying.

"That's why I think Jesus Christ only wanted to be born poor to show off. Afterward he saw that only the rich were any good. . . . But let's not talk about this anymore. What I said might be a really big sin."

He was so distraught that he didn't even look up from the horse's body, which he was now stroking.

* * *

Supper that Christmas Eve was so sad that I didn't even want to think. Everyone ate in silence, and Papa had only a little taste of the French toast. He hadn't shaved or anything. No one went to mass. The worst thing was that no one said anything to anyone. It was more like the Baby Jesus's funeral than his birth.

Papa fetched his hat and went out. He left without saying good-bye or wishing anyone Merry Christmas, in his sandals. Gran pulled out a handkerchief and dabbed her eyes and asked Uncle Edmundo to take her home. Uncle Edmundo put five tostões in my hand and five in Totoca's. Maybe he wanted to give us more but didn't have enough. Maybe, instead of giving it to us, he wished he could be giving it to his own children in the city. That's why I hugged him. I think it was the only hug of the evening. No one embraced or had anything nice to say. Mama went to her room. I'm sure it was to cry in secret. And everyone felt like doing the same. Lalá went to see off Uncle Edmundo and Gran at the gate, and when they walked away ever so slowly, she said, "They look like they're too old for life and tired of everything."

The saddest thing was that the church bell filled the night with happy voices. And some rockets shot up to the heavens for God to see how happy people were.

When we went back inside, Glória and Jandira were washing the dirty dishes, and Glória's eyes were red as if she'd cried her heart out.

She tried to hide it and said to me and Totoca, "It's time for children to go to bed."

She looked at us as she said it. She knew that there were no more children there. We were all big — big and sad, supping on the same tattered sadness.

Maybe it was all the fault of the dull lamplight that had replaced the light that the power company had cut off. Maybe.

The only happy one was the little king, who was fast asleep with his thumb in his mouth. I stood the little horse next to his bed. I couldn't resist gently stroking his hair. My voice was a vast river of tenderness.

"Pip-squeak."

When the whole house was dark, I said quietly, "The French toast was good, wasn't it, Totoca?"

"I don't know. I didn't have any."

"Why not?"

"I had something caught in my throat. Nothing would go down. . . . Let's sleep. Sleep makes you forget everything."

I started to get up, and Totoca could hear me moving around on the bed.

"Where're you going, Zezé?"

"I'm going to put my shoes outside the door."

"Don't. Best not to."

"I'm going to. You never know: maybe a miracle will happen. You know, Totoca, I'd love a present. Just one. But something new, just for me. . . ."

He rolled over and shoved his head under the pillow.

I called Totoca the minute I woke up.

"Let's go see! I say there is something."

"I wouldn't bother."

"Well, I'm going to."

I opened the bedroom door, and, to my disappointment, my shoes were empty. Totoca came over, rubbing his eyes.

"Didn't I tell you?"

A mixture of everything welled up in my soul. It was loathing, anger, and sadness. Unable to contain myself, I blurted out, "Having a poor father is awful!"

My eyes traveled from my shoes to a pair of sandals that were parked in front of me. Papa was standing there looking at us. His eyes were enormous with sadness. It looked like his eyes had grown so big — so big that they'd occupy the entire Cinema Bangu screen. There was so much hurt in his eyes that he couldn't have cried if he'd wanted to. He stood there looking at us for a minute that was endless, then walked past in silence. We stood there, frozen, unable to say a thing. He took his hat from the chest of drawers and left the house again. Only then did Totoca touch my arm.

"You're mean, Zezé. Mean as a snake. That's why . . ."

His voice faltered and he stopped.

"I didn't see him there."

"Mean. Heartless. You know Papa's been unemployed for a long time. That's why I couldn't swallow yesterday, looking at his face. One day you'll be a father, and you'll know how much it hurts at times like this."

Any more and I'd cry.

"But I didn't see him, Totoca. I didn't see . . ."

"Get away from me. You really are good for nothing. Go!"

I felt like racing down the street and clinging to Papa's legs, crying. Telling him I'd been mean—really, really mean. But I just stood there, not knowing what to do. I sat on the bed. And from there I stared at my shoes, in the same corner, as empty as could be. As empty as my heart, careening out of control.

Good God, why did I do that? Today of all days. Why did I have to be even meaner when everything was already so sad? How will I look at him at lunchtime? I won't even be able to swallow the fruit salad.

And in my mind, his big eyes, like a cinema screen, were glued to me, staring. I closed my eyes and still saw his big, big eyes. . . .

I tapped my shoe-shine box with my heel and had an idea. Maybe I could make Papa forgive me for being so mean.

I opened Totoca's box and borrowed a tin of black shoe polish because mine was running out. I didn't say a word to anyone. I walked sadly down the street, not feeling the weight of the box. It was as if I was walking over his eyes. Hurting inside his eyes.

It was very early, and adults were probably still asleep because of mass and supper the night before. The street was full of children showing off and comparing their toys. It made me feel even worse. They were all good children. None of them would ever do what I'd done.

I stopped near the Misery and Hunger, hoping to find a customer. The bar was open even on Christmas Day. It was no accident it had the nickname it did. People came in their pajamas, in slippers, in sandals — but real shoes, never.

I hadn't eaten breakfast and wasn't at all hungry. My pain was much greater than any hunger. I walked to Rua do Progresso. I circled the market. I sat on the sidewalk outside Seu Rozemberg's pastry shop and . . . nothing.

The hours ran into one another, and I didn't make a single tostão. But I had to. I had to.

It grew hotter and the strap was hurting my shoulder, so I had to change positions from time to time. I felt thirsty and went to get a drink at the fountain in the market.

I sat on the front step of the school, which I'd probably have to go to soon. I put down the box, discouraged. Leaning my head on my knees like a doll, I just sat there, feeling listless. Then I hid my face between my knees and covered it with my arms. Better to die than go home without getting what I wanted.

A shoe tapped on my box, and I heard a familiar friendly voice. "Hey, shoe shine, you won't make any money sleeping on the job."

I looked up, unable to believe it. It was Seu Coquinho, the doorman of the casino. He placed one shoe on the box, and I wiped it with my rag first, then wet the shoe and dried it off. Then I started carefully rubbing in the shoe polish.

"Could you please lift up your trouser leg, sir?"

He did as I asked.

"Working today, Zezé?"

"I've never needed to more."

"And how was Christmas?"

"It was OK."

I tapped the box with the brush, and he changed feet. I repeated the steps and then began to polish. When I finished, I tapped the box and he took his shoe off it.

"How much, Zezé?"

"Two tostões."

"Why only two? Everyone else charges four."

"I'll only be able to charge that much when I'm a really good shoe shine. But not now."

He handed me five tostões.

"Keep the change for Christmas. See you later."

"Merry Christmas, Seu Coquinho."

Maybe he'd come to get his shoes polished because of what had happened three days earlier.

The money in my pocket lifted my spirits a little, but it didn't last long. It was already after two in the afternoon, people were out and about, and still nothing. Not a single customer, not even to dust off their shoes and relieve themselves of a tostão.

I stood near a lamppost on the highway and shouted from time to time in my high-pitched voice:

"Shoe shine, mister? Shoe shine, sir? Get a shoe shine and help the poor at Christmas!"

A rich man's car stopped nearby. I took the opportunity to shout again, not at all hopeful.

"A helping hand, sir? To help the poor at Christmas."

The well-dressed woman and children in the back seat sat there staring and staring at me. The woman took pity on me.

"Poor little thing, so small and so poor. Give him something, Artur."

But the man was eyeing me suspiciously.

"That one there's a little delinquent, and a wily one at that. He's taking advantage of his size and the day."

"Well, I'm going to give him something anyway. Come here, son."

She opened her handbag and stuck her hand out the window.

"No, ma'am, thank you. I'm not lying. You only work on Christmas if you really have to."

I picked up my box, slung it over my shoulder,

and started walking slowly. I had no energy left to be angry.

But the car door opened and a little boy came running over to me.

"Here, take this. Mother said to say she doesn't think you're lying."

He shoved five tostões in my pocket and didn't even wait for me to thank him. . . . I just heard the noise of the car engine moving away.

Four hours had passed, and Papa's eyes were still tormenting me.

I started to make my way home. Ten tostões wasn't enough, but maybe the Misery and Hunger would give it to me for less or let me pay the difference another day.

Something caught my eye on the corner of a fence. It was a torn black woman's stocking. I bent over and picked it up. I pulled it over my hand, and the fabric became very thin. I put it in my box, thinking, *This'll make a good snake.* But I argued with myself. *Another day. Not today, no way . . .*

I came to the Villas-Boas family's house. It had

a large cemented-over front yard. Serginho was riding around the flower beds on a beautiful bicycle. I pressed my face against the fence to watch.

The bicycle was red with streaks of yellow and blue. The metal gleamed. Serginho saw me and began to show off. He went fast, sped around corners, and braked so hard the wheels squealed. Then he came over.

"Like it?"

"It's the most beautiful bike in the world."

"Come to the gate—you'll be able to see better."

Serginho was Totoca's age and in his class.

I was ashamed of my bare feet because he was wearing shiny shoes, white socks, and red suspenders. His shoes were so shiny, they reflected everything. Even Papa's eyes began to stare out of the shine at me. I gulped.

"S'up, Zezé? You're acting weird."

"Nothing. It's even more beautiful up close. You get it for Christmas?"

"Yep."

He climbed off the bike to talk and opened the gate.

"I got lots of stuff. A gramophone, three suits, a heap of storybooks, a huge box of colored pencils. A box full of games, a plane with a propeller that moves. Two boats with white sails . . ."

I lowered my head and remembered Baby Jesus, who only liked rich people, just as Totoca had said.

"What's wrong, Zezé?"

"Nothing."

"What about you? . . . Did you get lots of stuff?"

I shook my head, unable to reply.

"Nothing? Nothing at all?"

"This year we didn't have Christmas at my place. Papa's still out of work."

"It's not possible. Didn't you have nuts, wine?"

"Just French toast, which Gran made, and coffee."

Serginho looked thoughtful.

"Zezé, will you accept an invitation?"

I had a fair idea what it was. But even though my stomach was empty, I didn't feel like it.

"Let's go inside. Mama will fix you a plate. There's so much food, so many sweets . . ."

I didn't want to take the risk. I'd had a hard time

of it the last few days. I'd heard someone say more than once, "I've told you before not to bring street kids into the house."

"No, thank you very much."

"OK. What if I ask Mama to make a packet of nuts and things for you to take to your little brother—will you take it?"

"I can't. I have to finish work."

Only then did Serginho notice the shoe-shine box that I was sitting on.

"But no one gets their shoes shined on Christmas. . . ."

"I've been at it all day and I only made ten tostões, and half of it was people taking pity on me. I still need to make another two."

"What for, Zezé?"

"I can't say. But I really need it."

He smiled and had a generous idea.

"Want to shine mine? I'll give you ten tostões."

"I can't do that either. I don't charge friends."

"Well, what if I give you, that is, lend you, the two tostões?"

"Can I take a while to pay you back?"

"Whatever you like. You can even pay me in marbles."

"Then, yes."

He reached into his pocket and handed me the money.

"Don't worry about it, 'cause people gave me a lot of money. My piggy bank's full."

I ran my hand over the wheel of the bike.

"It's really beautiful."

"When you're bigger and learn how to ride, I'll let you take it for a spin, OK?"

"OK."

I charged off to the Misery and Hunger, my shoe-shine box jiggling.

I raced in like a hurricane, afraid it might be closing time.

"Have you still got those expensive cigarettes?"

Seu Misery and Hunger got two packs down when he saw the money in my hand.

"This isn't for you, is it, Zezé?"

A voice behind him said, "Are you mad? A child that size!"

Without turning, he replied, "You don't know this customer. This kid's capable of anything."

"It's for Papa."

I felt enormously happy as I turned the packs over in my hands.

"This one or this one?"

"It's up to you."

"I spent the day working to buy this Christmas present for Papa."

"Is that so, Zezé? And what did he give you?"

"Nothing, the poor fellow. He's still unemployed, you know."

He was moved. No one at the bar spoke.

"Which one would you like if it was you?"

"Both are nice. And any father would like a present like this."

"Then wrap this one up for me, please, sir."

He wrapped it up, but he looked a bit strange when he handed me the package, as if he wanted to say something but couldn't. I handed him the money and smiled.

"Thanks, Zezé."

"Merry Christmas to you, sir!"

I ran home.

Night had fallen. Only the lantern in the kitchen was on. Everyone had gone out, but Papa was sitting at the table staring vacantly at the wall, chin in hand, elbow on the table.

"Papa."

"What, son?" There wasn't a trace of resentment in his voice. "Where've you been all day?"

I showed him my shoe-shine box. Then I set it on the floor and pulled the package out of my pocket.

"Look, Papa, I bought you something nice."

He smiled, understanding how much it had cost.

"Do you like it? It was the nicest one they had."

He opened the pack and took a whiff of the cigarettes, smiling, but unable to say anything.

"Smoke one, Papa."

I went to the stove to get a match. I struck it and held it close to the cigarette in his mouth.

I stepped back to watch him take his first drag. And something began to well up in me. I threw the burnt match on the floor, feeling that I was bursting. Erupting on the inside. That enormous pain that had been threatening to erupt all day.

I looked at Papa. His unshaven face, his eyes.

"Papa . . . Papa . . ." was all I could say before tears and sobs got the better of my voice.

He spread his arms wide and hugged me tenderly.

"Don't cry, son. You're going to have a lot to cry about in life, if you go on being so emotional . . ."

"I didn't mean to, Papa . . . I didn't mean to say . . . *that*."

"I know. I know. I wasn't upset, because deep down you were right."

He rocked me in his arms a little more. Then he lifted my face and dried it with a tea towel that was lying nearby.

"That's better."

I raised my hands and stroked his face. I passed them lightly over his eyes, trying to put them back where they belonged, away from that big cinema screen. I was afraid that if I didn't, those eyes were going to follow me for the rest of my life.

"I'm going to finish off my cigarette."

Still choked up, I spluttered, "You know, Papa, when you want to beat me, I'll never complain again. You just go ahead and do it . . ."

"Hey, hey, Zezé."

He put me and the rest of my sobs down and got a plate from the cupboard.

"Glória saved a bit of fruit salad for you."

I couldn't swallow. He sat down and fed it to me in small spoonfuls.

"It's OK now, isn't it, son?"

I nodded, but the first spoonfuls tasted salty. It was my last few tears, which were taking a long time to go away.

CHAPTER FOUR

The Little Bird, School, and the Flower

New house. New life and simple hopes, hopes pure and simple.

On moving day, off I went between Seu Aristides and his helper, perched on the top of the cart, as happy as the day was hot.

When it left the unpaved street and turned onto the Rio–São Paulo Highway, it was marvelous. The cart slid smoothly along now. It was lovely.

A beautiful car passed us.

"There goes Manuel Valadares's car."

When we were crossing the intersection at Rua dos Açudes, a distant whistle filled the morning.

"Hey, Seu Aristides. There goes the Mangaratiba."

"You know everything, don't you?"

"I know the sound it makes."

The only sound was hooves going *clip-clop* on the highway. I noticed that the cart wasn't very new. On the contrary. But it was sturdy and affordable. Two more trips and we'd have moved all our junk. The donkey didn't look too strong. But I wanted to be nice.

"This is a fine cart, Seu Aristides."

"It does the job."

"And that's a fine donkey. What's his name?"

"Gypsy."

He wasn't in the mood for chitchat.

"Today's a big day for me. This is my first time on a cart. And I've seen Manuel Valadares's car and heard the Mangaratiba."

Silence. Nothing.

"Seu Aristides, is the Mangaratiba the most important train in Brazil?"

"No. It's the most important one on this line."

It was no use. How hard it was to understand grown-ups sometimes!

When we got to the house, I handed him the key and tried to be polite: "Would you like me to help with anything, sir?"

"You can help by staying out of our way. Go play and we'll call you when it's time to head back."

So I did.

"Pinkie, now we're always going to live near each other. I'm going to dress you up so beautifully that no other tree will hold a candle to you. You know, Pinkie, just now I rode on a cart so big and smooth that it felt like one of those coaches that you see in the cinema. Look, everything I find out, I'll come tell you, OK?"

I went over to the long grass growing in the ditch and looked at the dirty water running through it.

"What did we decide the river was going to be called the other day?"

"The Amazon."

"That's right. The Amazon. Downstream it must be full of canoes, right, Pinkie?"

"Tell me about it! It must be."

We'd barely started chatting, and there was Seu Aristides closing up the house and calling me.

"You staying or coming with us?"

"I'll stay here. Mama and my sisters must be on their way by now."

And I went around examining every little detail of the place.

In the beginning, out of shyness, or because I wanted to make a good impression on the neighbors, I was well behaved. But one afternoon I stuffed the black stocking, rolled it in twine, and cut out the tip of the toe. Then I tied a long piece of kite string to the place where the toe had been. From a distance, if I pulled slowly on it, it looked like a snake, and in the dark it would work like a charm.

At night everyone went about their own business. It was as if the new house had changed everyone's spirits. There was a cheerfulness in the family that hadn't been present for a long time.

I waited quietly by the gate. The street was dimly lit by the lampposts, and the hedges cast shadows into corners. There must have been people working overtime at the factory, and overtime never went past eight o'clock. It rarely went past nine. I thought about the factory for a moment. I didn't like it. Its sad morning whistle was even uglier at five o'clock. The factory was a dragon that gobbled up people every morning and spewed them out, very tired, at night. I also didn't like it because of what Mr. Scottfield had done to Papa.

Along came a woman. She was holding a handbag and had a parasol under her arm. You could hear the *clickety-clack* of her heels on the pavement.

I ran to hide behind the gate and tested the string attached to the snake. It obeyed. It was perfect. Then I crouched down in the shadow of the hedge with the string in my fingers. Her heels drew closer and closer, then even closer and *zip*! I tugged on the string. It slid slowly across the middle of the street.

I wasn't expecting what happened next. The woman screamed so loudly that she roused the street. She threw her handbag and parasol in the air and clasped her belly, screaming all the while.

"Help! Help! A snake! Someone help me!"

Doors were flung open, and I dropped everything, bolted down the side of the house, and entered through the kitchen. I took the lid off the laundry basket and climbed inside, pulling the lid over the top. My heart was pounding in fright, and I could still hear the woman screaming.

"Oh, my God, I'm six months pregnant and I'm going to lose my baby."

Not only did a shiver run down my spine, but I also began to tremble.

The neighbors took her inside, but the sobs and laments continued.

"Good Lord, good Lord. A snake of all things— I'm terrified of them."

"Have a little orange blossom water. There, there, stay calm. The men have gone after it with sticks, an ax, and a lantern to light the way."

What a big fuss over a little stocking snake! But the worst part was that my family had also gone to see what was going on. Jandira, Mama, and Lalá.

"That's not a snake. It's an old stocking."

In my fright I had forgotten to remove the "snake." I was done for.

Attached to the snake was the string, and the string led into our yard.

Three familiar voices chimed at once: "It was him!"

It wasn't the snake they were after now. They looked under the bed. Nothing. They passed by me, and I didn't even breathe. They went out the back to look in the outhouse.

Then Jandira had an idea.

"I think I know where he is!"

She lifted the lid off the laundry basket, and I was hauled out to the dining room by the ears.

Mama beat me hard this time. While her sandal whistled through the air, I really had to holler so it wouldn't hurt so much and she'd stop hitting me sooner.

"You little pest! You have no idea how hard it is to get around when you're six months pregnant. Now, straight to bed, you little wretch."

I left, scratching my backside, and lay down on my belly. Luckily Papa had gone out to play cards. I lay there in the dark sniffling and thinking that going to bed was the best way to get over a paddling.

* * *

I got up early the next day. I had two very important things to do: first, go have a look around, very
casually. If the snake was still there, I'd get it and
hide it in my shirt. I could still use it somewhere else.
But it wasn't. It'd be hard to find another stocking as
snake-like as that one.

I turned and started off to Gran's house. I needed
to talk to Uncle Edmundo.

I knew it was still early for a retired person. I
wanted to catch him before he went out to buy a lottery ticket — or "place a bet," as he called it — and
pick up the newspapers. I was right. He was in the
living room playing a new kind of solitaire.

"Morning, Uncle!"

He didn't answer. He was pretending to be deaf.
Back at home, everyone said that he did that when
he wasn't interested in the conversation.

But never with me. In fact (how I liked saying "in
fact"!), he was never very deaf around me. I tugged
on his shirtsleeve and, as always, thought his black-
and-white-checkered suspenders looked very fine.

"Ah! It's you . . ."

He was pretending he hadn't seen me.

"What's the name of this solitaire, Uncle?"

"It's called the Clock."

"It's pretty."

I already knew all the cards in the deck. I just wasn't too keen on jacks. I don't know why, but they looked like they were the servants of the kings.

"You know, Uncle, I've come to tell you something."

"I'm just about finished. When I'm done, we can talk."

But soon he shuffled all the cards up.

"Did you win?"

"No."

He made a little pile of cards and set it aside.

"OK, Zezé, if this something has to do with money," he said, rubbing his fingers together, "I'm ready."

"Haven't you got one little tostão for me to buy a marble with?"

He smiled.

"I might have one little tostão. Who knows?"

He was about to put his hand in his pocket, but I stopped him.

"Just kidding, Uncle, that's not it."

"Well, then, what is it?"

I could tell my "precociousness" amused him, especially after I taught myself to read.

"I'd like to know something very important. Do you know how to sing without singing?"

"I'm not sure I follow."

"Like this," and I sang a verse of "The Little House." "I can do it all inside without singing on the outside."

"That's humming," he said, laughing, unsure where I was going with it.

"Look, Uncle, when I was little, I thought I had a little bird inside me that sang. It was the bird that sang."

"Well, then. It's wonderful that you have a little bird like that."

"You don't understand. It's just that now I'm not so sure about the bird. What about when I speak and see on the inside?"

He understood and laughed at my confusion.

"I'll tell you what it is, Zezé. It means you're growing. And when you grow, this thing that you say speaks and sees is called thinking. And thinking is what makes you reach the age I said you'd be reaching soon."

"The age of reason?"

"It's good that you remember. Then something wonderful happens. Our thinking grows and grows and takes over our heads and our hearts. It lives in our eyes and in every part of our lives."

"Right. And what about the little bird?"

"The little bird was made by God to help children discover things. Then when the child no longer needs it, he gives it back to God. And God puts it in another intelligent boy like you. Isn't that beautiful?"

I laughed happily because I was thinking.

"It is. I'll be going now."

"Still want that tostão?"

"Not today. I'm going to be very busy."

I set off down the street thinking about everything. But I remembered something that made me really sad. Totoca used to have a beautiful finch. It was tame and perched on his finger when he changed its birdseed. He could even leave the door open, and it wouldn't fly away. One day Totoca forgot him out in the sun. And the hot sun killed him. I remembered Totoca holding him in his hand, crying—crying and holding the dead bird to his cheek. Then he said, "I'll never keep a bird in a cage again."

I was with him and said, "Me neither, Totoca."

When I got home, I went straight to Pinkie.

"Sweetie, I've come to do something," I said.

"What?"

"Can we wait a bit?"

"OK."

I sat down and leaned my head against his trunk.

"What are we waiting for, Zezé?"

"For a really pretty cloud to float past in the sky."

"What for?"

"I'm going to let my little bird go. Yes, I'm going to. I don't need it anymore."

We sat there staring at the sky.

"Is it that one, Pinkie?"

The cloud came drifting along slowly, really big, like a white leaf with torn edges.

"That's the one, Pinkie."

I stood and unbuttoned my shirt. I felt it leaving my skinny chest.

"Fly away, little bird. Really high. Go way up high and perch on God's finger. God is going to take you to another little boy, and you are going to sing beautifully for him just as you always have for me. Bye-bye, my sweet little bird!"

I felt an emptiness inside that was endless.

"Look, Zezé. It perched on the cloud's finger."

"I see it."

I leaned my head against Pinkie's heart and watched the cloud drift away.

"I never mistreated him. . . ."

Then I turned my face and pressed it against Pinkie's branch.

"Sweetie."

"What?"

"Is it wrong for me to cry?"

"It's never wrong to cry, silly. Why?"

"I don't know, I'm still not used to it. It feels like my cage inside is too empty now."

* * *

Glória woke me up early.

"Show me your fingernails."

I showed her my hands and she approved them.

"Now your ears. Ew, Zezé!"

She took me to the washtub, wet a cloth with soap on it, and rubbed off the filth.

"I've never seen someone who claims to be an Apinajé warrior who's always dirty! Go get your shoes on while I find some decent clothes for you to wear."

She went to my drawer and rummaged around. And she rummaged around some more. And the more she rummaged, the less she found. All my trousers had holes in them or were torn, patched, or darned.

"You don't need to say a thing. If anyone ever saw this drawer, they'd know what a terror you are. Put this one on; it's not as bad as the rest."

And off we went for the "wonderful" discovery that I was about to make.

School. As we approached, we saw a whole bunch of people taking children by the hand to enroll them.

"Now, don't look sad or forget anything, Zezé."

We took a seat in a room full of children who were all peering at one another. Then our turn came, and we went into the headmistress's office.

"Is he your little brother?"

"Yes, ma'am. Mama couldn't come because she works in the city."

She looked at me for a long time, and her eyes were big and black because her glasses were very thick. Funny thing was, she had a man's mustache. She must have been the headmistress because of that.

"Isn't he too young?"

"He's small for his age. But he already knows how to read."

"How old are you, boy?"

"On the twenty-sixth of February, I turn six, ma'am."

"Very well. Let's fill in your application. First your parents' names."

Glória told her Papa's name. But when she got to Mama's name, she just said, "Estefânia de Vasconcelos."

I couldn't help myself and corrected her, "Estefânia Apinajé de Vasconcelos."

"Excuse me?"

Glória blushed a little.

"It's Apinajé. Mama's parents were Indians."

I puffed up with pride because I must have been the only kid with an Indian name at that school.

Then Glória signed a paper and stopped, hesitant.

"Is there something else?"

"I'd like to know about the uniforms. . . . You see . . . Papa is unemployed and we're very poor."

Which was proven when the headmistress asked me to turn around so she could get an idea of my size and saw my patches.

She wrote a number on a piece of paper and sent us inside to look for Dona Eulália.

Dona Eulália was also surprised at how small I was. The smallest size she had was so big I was drowning in it.

"This is the smallest I've got, but it's too big. What a tiny child!"

"I can take it up."

She gave us two uniforms and we left. I was pleased with the present and imagined Pinkie's face when he saw me in my new school clothes.

As the days went by, I told him everything. What it was like, what went on there.

"They ring a big bell. But not as big as the church bell. You know, right? Everyone goes into the main courtyard and looks for the place where their teacher is. She makes us line up in fours, and everyone walks into the classroom like little lambs. We all sit at desks with lids that open and close, and we put our stuff inside them. I'm going to have to learn a bunch of anthems, because the teacher said that to be a good Brazilian and a "patriot," we have to know the anthem of our land. When I learn it, I'll sing it to you, OK, Pinkie?"

And along came a world in which everything was new and had to be discovered afresh.

"Hey, where are you going with that flower?"

The girl was clean, and her schoolbooks had nice covers. Her hair was in braids.

"I'm taking it to my teacher."

"Why?"

"Because she likes them. And all hardworking girls should take flowers to their teachers."

"Can boys take them too?"

"If you like your teacher, you can."

"Really?"

"Yes."

No one had taken a single flower to my teacher, Dona Cecília Paim. It must have been because she was ugly. If she didn't have a spot on her eye, she wouldn't have been so ugly. But she was the only one who would sometimes give me a tostão to buy a pastry at playtime.

I started peering into the other classrooms, and all the glasses on the teachers' desks had flowers in them. Only my teacher's glass remained empty.

The biggest adventure was something else.

"Guess what, Pinkie. Today I went for a piggyback ride."

"You rode a horse?"

"No, silly. When the cars drive past the school really slowly, you grab the tire on the back and go for a piggyback. When they're going to turn onto another street, they slow down to see if there are any cars coming, and you jump off. But carefully. 'Cause if you jump off when it's going fast, your bum'll go splat on the ground and your arms'll get all smashed up."

I'd chatter away to him about everything that happened in class and on the playground. You had to see how he puffed up with pride when I told him that Dona Cecília Paim said I was the one who read the best. The best "readerer." I wasn't exactly sure about that and decided that at the first opportunity I would ask Uncle Edmundo if I really was a "readerer."

"But about the piggyback, Pinkie. Just to give you an idea of what it's like, it's almost as good as riding on one of your branches."

"But with me you're not in any danger."

"Is that so? What about when you gallop wildly over the western plains when we go bison and buffalo hunting? Have you forgotten?"

He had to agree because he didn't know how to argue with me and win.

"But there's one, Pinkie. . . . There's one that

no one dares to piggyback on. Know which one it is? That big car that belongs to Manuel Valadares. How's that for an ugly name? Manuel Valadares . . ."

"Yes, it is. But I'm thinking something."

"You think I don't know what you're thinking? I know, yes. But not yet. Let me practice more. . . . Then I'll give it a try. . . ."

The days went past with great cheer. One morning I showed up with a flower for my teacher. She was moved and said that I was a gentleman.

"Do you know what that is, Pinkie?"

"A gentleman is someone who is very polite, like a prince."

And every day I developed more and more of a taste for my lessons and applied myself even harder. There were never any complaints about me from the school. Glória said that I had left my little devil in the drawer and become another child.

"Do you think it's true, Pinkie?"

"I guess so."

"Is that so? 'Cause I was going to tell you a secret, but now I'm not going to."

I left in a huff. But he didn't worry about it much because he knew I never stayed mad for long.

The secret was going to happen at night, and I was so anxious that my heart was almost leaping out of my chest. It took ages for the factory whistle to go off and the people to go past. Night took a long time to arrive in summer. Even dinnertime never came. I stayed at the gate watching and didn't have a single thought about snakes or anything else. I sat there waiting for Mama. Even Jandira found it odd and asked if I had a stomachache because I'd eaten unripe fruit.

Mama's silhouette appeared at the street corner. It was her! No one in the world looked like her. I jumped up and ran.

"Hello, Mama," I said, kissing her hand.

Even in the poorly lit street, I could see that her face looked tired.

"Did you work a lot today, Mama?"

"Yes, son. It was so hot at the loom that no one could bear it."

"Give me your bag. You're tired."

I took her bag with her empty lunch box in it.

"Did you get up to much mischief today?"

"Only a bit, Mama."

"Why did you wait at the gate for me?"

She was trying to guess.

"Mama, do you love me just a little?"

"I love you as much as I love your brothers and sisters. Why?"

"Mama, remember Nardinho? The hippo's nephew?"

"Yes," she said, laughing.

"His mother made a fine suit for him. It's green with white stripes. It has a waistcoat that buttons up to the neck. But he's grown out of it. And he doesn't have a younger brother who can use it. And he wants to sell it. Can you buy it?"

"Oh, child! Things are so difficult!"

"But he said you can pay in two installments. And it isn't expensive. It won't even cover the cost of making it."

I was repeating Jacob the moneylender's words. She was quiet, doing the math.

"Mama, I'm the hardest-working pupil in my class. The teacher says I'm going to get a distinction.

Please buy it for me, Mama. I've haven't had new clothes for such a long time. . . ."

Her silence was unsettling me.

"Look, Mama, if you don't, I'm never going to have my poet's clothes. Lalá can make me a tie with a big bow like this out of a piece of silk she's got. . . ."

"OK, son. I'll do a week of overtime, and I'll buy you the suit."

Then I kissed her hand and walked next to her with my face pressed to her hand until we were inside the house.

That was how I got my poet's clothes. I looked so smart that Uncle Edmundo took me to have my photograph taken.

School. Flower. Flower. School . . .

Everything was going fine when Godofredo came into the classroom. He excused himself and asked to speak to Dona Cecília Paim. All I know is that he pointed at the flower in the glass. Then he left. She looked at me sadly.

When class was over, she called me over.

"I'd like to talk to you about something, Zezé. Just a minute."

She rummaged in her handbag for a long time. I could tell she didn't really want to talk to me and was searching for courage among her things. Finally, she decided.

"Godofredo told me something very bad about you, Zezé. Is it true?"

I nodded.

"About the flower? It's true, miss."

"What exactly did you do?"

"I woke up early and stopped by Serginho's front garden. When the gate wasn't closed all the way, I slipped in and stole a flower. But they have so many that it won't be missed."

"Yes. But it's not right. You shouldn't do it anymore. It's not serious, but it's a kind of theft."

"No, it isn't, Dona Cecília. Doesn't the world belong to God? Doesn't everything in the world belong to God? Then flowers belong to God too . . ."

She was surprised by my logic.

"It was the only way, miss. There's no garden at

my place. Flowers cost money. . . . And I didn't want the glass on your desk to always be empty."

She gulped.

"Don't you give me money from time to time, to buy a pastry?"

"I could give it to you every day. But you disappear. . . ."

"I couldn't accept it every day. . . ."

"Why not?"

"Because there are other poor children who don't bring anything to eat either."

She pulled a handkerchief out of her bag and discreetly dabbed her eyes with it.

"Don't you see Little Owl?"

"Who's Little Owl?"

"The little black girl who's my size and her mother rolls her hair up in little buns and ties string around them."

"Oh, yes, you mean Dorotília."

"Yes, ma'am. Dorotília is even poorer than me. And the other girls don't like to play with her because she's black and poor. So she always stays in a corner. I share the pastry that you give me with her."

This time she stood there with the handkerchief pressed to her nose for a long time.

"Every now and then, instead of giving it to me, you could give it to her. Her mama is a washer-woman, and she has eleven children. All still young. Gran gives them some rice and beans every Saturday to help them out. And I share my pastry with her because Mama taught us that we should share the little we have with those who have even less."

Tears were rolling down her face now.

"I didn't mean to make you cry. I promise not to steal flowers anymore, and I'm going to study even harder."

"It's not that, Zezé. Come here."

She took my hands in hers.

"I want you to promise me something, because you have a beautiful heart, Zezé."

"I promise, but I don't want to mislead you, ma'am. I don't have a beautiful heart. You say that because you don't know what I'm like at home."

"It doesn't matter. To me you do. From now on I don't want you to bring me any more flowers. Only if they're given to you. Promise?"

"I promise. But what about the glass? Will it always be empty?"

"This glass will never be empty. Whenever I look at it, I'll always see the most beautiful flower in the world. And I'll think: My best pupil gave me that flower. OK?"

Now she laughed. She let go of my hands and spoke sweetly.

"Now off you go, heart of gold . . ."

CHAPTER FIVE

"*In a Prison I Hope You Die*"

The first very useful thing that we learned at school was the days of the week. And once I had mastered the days of the week, I knew that *he* came on Tuesday. Then I also discovered that one Tuesday he would go to the streets on the other side of the station and the next he would come to our side.

That's why that Tuesday I skipped class. I didn't want Totoca to know, or I'd have to pay him marbles not to say anything at home. Because it was early and *he* wouldn't arrive until the church bells chimed nine, I went for a stroll through the streets. Streets that weren't dangerous, of course. First I stopped at the church and took a look at the saints. I felt a little scared seeing the still statues, surrounded by candles. The winking candles made the saints wink too. I wasn't sure if it would be nice to be a saint and have to be really still all the time.

I went for a walk around the sacristy, and Seu Zacarias was taking the old candles out of the candleholders and putting new ones in them. There was a pile of stubs on the table.

"Good morning, Seu Zacarias."

He stopped, moved his glasses to the tip of his nose, sniffed, turned around, and replied, "Good morning, son."

"Would you like me to help you?"

I couldn't stop looking at the candle stubs.

"Only if you want to get in the way. Didn't you go to school today?" he said, returning to work.

"I did. But the teacher didn't come. She had a toothache."

"Oh!"

He turned around and moved his glasses to the tip of his nose again.

"How old are you, child?"

"Five. No, six. No, I'm five."

"Well, is it five or six?"

I thought about school and lied.

"Six."

"Well, six is a good age to start Catechism classes."

"Am I allowed?"

"Why not? All you have to do is come every Thursday, at three o'clock in the afternoon. Want to come?"

"That depends. If you give me the candle stubs, I'll come."

"What do you want candle stubs for?"

The devil had already given me a nudge. I lied again.

"It's to wax my kite string to make it stronger."

"Then take them."

I gathered up the stubs and stuffed them in my satchel with my schoolbooks and marbles. I was deliriously happy.

"Thank you very much, Seu Zacarias."

"Don't forget, now. Thursday."

I raced out of there. It was early; there was time. I hurried to the front of the casino and, when no one was coming, crossed the street and rubbed the stubs of wax on the sidewalk as quickly as possible. Then I ran back and sat down to wait on the sidewalk outside one of the casino's four closed doors. I wanted to see from a distance who would be the first to slip.

I was just about to give up waiting when, suddenly, *plop*! My heart leapt. Dona Corinha, Nanzeazena's mother, walked through her gate with a handkerchief and a book, and set off for the church.

"Holy Mother of God!"

Dona Corinha, of all people—she was a friend of Mama's, and Nanzeazena was good friends with Glória. I didn't want to watch. I bolted for the corner and stopped to look. She had come crashing to the ground and was cursing.

People gathered around to see if she was hurt, but judging by the way she was cursing, she must have only gotten a few scratches.

"It was those little delinquents."

I let out a sigh of relief. But I wasn't so relieved that I failed to feel a hand taking hold of my satchel.

"That was your doing, wasn't it, Zezé?"

Seu Orlando-Hair-on-Fire. He of all people, who'd been our neighbor for many years. I couldn't speak.

"Was it or wasn't it?"

"Promise not to tell my parents?"

"I'm not going to tell. But look here, Zezé. I'll let it go this time 'cause that woman's a real gossip. But don't do it again because someone could break a leg."

I made the most obedient face in the world, and he let me go.

I headed back to the market, waiting for *him* to arrive. But before that, I stopped by Seu Rozemberg's pastry shop, smiled, and said, "Good day, Seu Rozemberg."

He wished me good day drily and didn't offer me a sweet. Son of a bitch! He only gave me sweets when I was with Lalá.

"Here he comes."

The clock clanged nine o'clock. He came like

he always did. I followed him from a distance. He turned onto Rua do Progresso and stopped on the corner. He put his bag on the ground and threw his jacket over his left shoulder. What a nice checked shirt! *When I'm a grown-up,* I thought, *I'll only wear shirts like that.* He had a red kerchief around his neck, and his hat was tipped back. Then he boomed in his deep voice that filled the street with cheer, "Gather 'round, my good people! Come hear what's new!"

His Bahian accent was lovely too.

"This week's hits: 'Claudionor'! 'Pardon'! . . . Chico Viola's latest song. Vicente Celestino's latest success. Come learn it — it's all the rage."

His singsong way of speaking fascinated me.

I wanted him to sing "the bit about Fanny." He always sang it, and I wanted to learn. When he got to the part that goes "In a prison I hope you die," it was so beautiful I even got goose pimples. He filled his lungs and sang "Claudionor."

> *I went to dance samba in the favela*
> *A girl looked at me and said, Hey there, big fella*
> *But I didn't go, my lust unfulfilled*

Her husband was strong, I could've been killed . . .
I don't want to be like Claudionor
To support his family, became a stevedore . . ."

He would stop and announce:

"Brochures with song lyrics for all pockets, from one to four tostões. Sixty new tunes! The latest tangos."

Then he'd come to the bit I'd been waiting for. Fanny.

"One day while she was busy with chores
He stabbed her to death behind closed doors
For the crime of being a tart . . ."

(Then his voice would grow so soft and sweet, it could have melted the hardest of hearts.)

"Poor, poor Fanny, who had a good heart
I swear to God you'll have reason to cry
IN A PRISON I HOPE YOU DIE
He stabbed her to death for being a tart
Poor, poor Fanny, who had a good heart."

People would come out of their houses to buy brochures, but not before studying them all to see which took their fancy. By this time I couldn't stop following him because of Fanny.

He turned to me with an enormous smile.

"Want one, boy?"

"No, sir. I don't have any money."

"I could tell."

He picked up his bag and strolled a little farther down the street, shouting, "The waltzes 'Pardon,' 'Smoking, I Wait,' and 'Bye-Bye Boys.' The tangos that are even more popular than 'Night of Kings.' In the city, everyone's singing 'Heavenly Light.' It's a beauty. Listen to the lyrics!"

And he sang:

"The light in your eyes is heavenly
I do believe that I can see
The glow of stars in constellations
Your eyes a well of temptations
Stare into my eyes and see
What moonlit love has done to me
And just how wretched love can be . . ."

He made a few more announcements, sold a few more brochures, and noticed me again. He stopped and beckoned me over with a finger.

"C'mere, finch."

I obeyed, smiling.

"Are you going to stop following me or not?"

"No, sir. Nobody in the world sings as beautifully as you."

He was flattered and a little disarmed. I was getting somewhere.

"But I can't go anywhere without you following me."

"It's just that I wanted to see if you sing better than Vicente Celestino and Chico Viola. And you do."

He flashed a broad grin.

"And have you heard them, finch?"

"Yes, sir. On a gramophone at Dr. Adaucto Luz's house, with his son."

"Then the gramophone must be old or the needle broken."

"No, sir. It was a brand-new gramophone that had just arrived. You really do sing a lot better. In fact, I was thinking something."

"What?"

"I'll follow you everywhere. You teach me how much each brochure costs. Then you sing and I sell the brochures. Everyone likes to buy from a child."

"Not a bad idea, finch. But one thing. If you come along, you come 'cause you want to. I can't pay you anything."

"But I don't want anything."

"Why's that?"

"Well, I really like to sing. I like to learn. And I think the song about Fanny is the most beautiful thing in the world. Now, if you end up selling lots, you could take an old brochure that nobody wants to buy and give it to me to give to my sister."

He took off his hat and scratched his head where his hair was flattened down.

"I have an older sister named Glória, and I'd give it to her. That's all."

"OK, then."

And we went along, singing and selling. He sang and I learned as I went.

When it was noon, he eyed me a little suspiciously. "Aren't you going home for lunch?"

"Only when we finish our work."

He scratched his head again.

"Come with me."

We sat in a bar on Rua Ceres, and he retrieved a big sandwich from the bottom of his bag. He pulled a knife out of his waistband. A scary-looking knife. He cut off a piece of his sandwich and gave it to me. Then he had a sip of cachaça and ordered two lemonades. As he ate his sandwich, he studied me with his eyes and his eyes were very content.

"Y'know, finch," he said with a drawl. "You're bringing me good luck. I've a row of potbellied young 'uns, and I never thought to get one of 'em to give me a hand."

He took a long sip of lemonade.

"How old are you?"

"Five. Six . . . Five."

"Five or six?"

"I still haven't turned six."

"Well, you're a nice, intelligent little boy."

"Does that mean we can meet up again next Tuesday?"

He laughed.

"If you wish."

"I do. But I'm going to have to arrange it with my sister. She'll understand. Actually, it's good, 'cause I've never been to the other side of the tracks."

"How do you know I go there?"

"I wait for you every Tuesday, sir. One Tuesday you come and the next one you don't. So I figured you go to the other side of the tracks."

"Clever boy! What's your name?"

"Zezé."

"I'm Ariovaldo. Shake."

He took my hand in his calloused hands so we'd be friends until death.

It wasn't hard to convince Glória.

"But, Zezé, once a week? What about school?"

I showed her my notebook, and my handwriting was all neat and meticulous. My grades were excellent. I did the same with my math book.

"And I'm the best at reading, Gló."

Even then she wasn't sure.

"What we're studying now we'll be studying for

the next six months, repeating the same thing over and over. Those donkeys take ages to learn."

She laughed.

"What a way to talk, Zezé."

"It's true, Glória, I learn much more from the singing. Want to see how many new things I've learned? Afterward Uncle Edmundo told me what they meant. *Stevedore, constellation, temptation,* and *wretched.* And on top of it all, I'll bring you a brochure of song lyrics every week and teach you the most beautiful songs in the world."

"Right. But there's just one thing. What do we tell Papa when he notices that you don't come home for lunch every Tuesday?"

"He won't. But if he asks, we lie. You say I went to have lunch at Gran's place. That I went to take a message to Nanzeazena and stayed for lunch."

Holy Mary! Just as well it was only pretend because if Nanzeazena's mother, Dona Corinha, found out what I'd done!

Glória ended up agreeing because she knew it was a way to keep me out of mischief, and so avoid beatings. And it was nice to sit under the trees with her on Wednesday, teaching her to sing.

I couldn't wait for Tuesdays to come. I would go wait for Seu Ariovaldo at the train station. When he didn't miss his train, he got there at eight-thirty.

I'd wander around, looking at everything. I liked to go to the pastry shop and watch the people coming down the stairs from the station. It was a good place to shine shoes. But Glória never let me because the police would chase us and take our boxes. And there were the trains, too. I could only go with Seu Ariovaldo if he gave me his hand, even if it was to take the footbridge to the other side.

Then he'd arrive, all flustered. After the song about Fanny, he was convinced that I knew what the people liked to buy.

We'd go sit on the wall of the station, across from the factory garden, and he'd open the brochure and show me the song, singing the first bit. When I didn't think it was good, he'd find another one.

"This one's new: 'Spoiled.'"

He sang it.

"Sing it again."

He repeated the last verse.

"That's the one, Seu Ariovaldo, plus 'Fanny' and the tangos; we're going to sell out."

And we'd go through the dusty, sunlit streets. We were the joyful birds who confirmed that summer was coming. His big, beautiful voice opened the window of the morning.

"The hit of the week, the month, the year: 'Spoiled,' recorded by Chico Viola."

> *"The full moon casts a silver sheen*
> *On the mountain, lush and green*
> *The serenader's trusty strings*
> *His love to the window bring.*
>
> *A heartfelt tune is gently spun*
> *Sweet lyre deftly plucked and strummed*
> *The crooner opens the floodgates*
> *to all his lovesick heart's dictates . . ."*

Then he'd pause a moment, nod twice, and I would come in with my pure little voice.

"No fairer vision ever seen
You are my light, you are my queen
If up to me, you'll never toil
Clever girl, you'll be spoiled."

You should have seen it! Girls would come running to buy brochures. Gentlemen, people of all ages and types. I really liked selling the ones that cost four or five tostões. When it was a woman, I knew what to do.

"Here's your change, ma'am."

"Keep it and buy yourself a sweet."

I was even beginning to talk like Seu Ariovaldo.

At noon we'd head into the first tavern we saw and —*chomp, chomp, chomp* — devour his sandwich, sometimes with an orange soda, sometimes a red one.

Then I'd stick my hand into my change pocket and spread it out on the table.

"Here, Seu Ariovaldo."

And I'd push the coins toward him. He'd smile and say, "You're a good kid, Zezé."

"Seu Ariovaldo," I asked him one day. "Why did you used to call me finch?"

"Back in Bahia, where I'm from, it means a little kid, a small child."

He scratched his head and covered his mouth to burp. Then he excused himself and took a toothpick to clean his teeth. The money stayed where it was.

"I've been thinking, Zezé. From now on you can keep the tips. After all, we're a duo now."

"What's a duo?"

"When two people sing together."

"Then can I buy a sweet?"

"It's your money. You can do what you want with it."

"Thanks, champ."

He laughed at the imitation. Now I was the one eating the sweet and looking at him.

"Am I really a duo?"

"You are now."

"Then let me sing the part about Fanny's heart. You sing loudly, and I'll join you in the bit about the heart, with the sweetest voice in the world."

"That's not a bad idea, Zezé."

"So, after lunch, let's start with 'Fanny,' 'cause it's really good luck."

And under the blazing sun, we went back to work.

We were in the middle of "Fanny" when disaster struck. Along came Dona Maria da Penha, looking all prim under her parasol, her face white with rice powder. She stopped and stood listening to us sing. Seu Ariovaldo saw tragedy coming and gave me a nudge to walk as I sang.

But I was so caught up in Fanny's heart that I paid no attention.

Dona Maria da Penha closed her parasol and stood there tapping the toe of her shoe with it. When I finished, she scowled angrily and exclaimed, "My, my. What an immoral song for a child to be singing."

"There's nothing immoral about my work, ma'am. Any honest work is work, and I am not ashamed of it!"

I'd never seen Seu Ariovaldo so annoyed. Maria da Penha was looking for a fight, and she got it.

"Is that child your son?"

"No, ma'am, 'fraid not."

"Your nephew, a relative?"

"Nope."

"How old is he?"

"Six."

She sized me up with a doubtful expression and continued. "Are you not ashamed to be exploiting a young child?"

"I'm not exploiting him at all, ma'am. He sings with me 'cause he wants to and 'cause he enjoys it. And I pay him, don't I?"

I nodded. I was loving the fight. I felt like head-butting her in the belly to see the noise she'd make when she hit the ground. *Boom!*

"Well, I'll have you know I am going to do something about this. I am going to speak to the priest. I'm going to child welfare. I'm going to the police."

Then her mouth snapped shut, and her eyes opened wide with fear. Ariovaldo had pulled out his enormous knife and taken a step toward her. She looked like she was about to throw a fit.

"Well, go ahead, ma'am. But go quickly. I'm a good man, but I do like to cut out the tongues of tongue-wagging witches who stick their noses in where they're not wanted. . . ."

She tottered off, as stiff as a broomstick, and

once at a distance turned and pointed her parasol.

"You'll see!"

"Skedaddle, you shooshy old witch!"

She opened her parasol and disappeared down the street, stiff as could be.

In the late afternoon, Seu Ariovaldo was counting the profits.

"We sold out, Zezé. You were right. You bring me good luck."

I remembered Dona Maria da Penha.

"Do you think she's going to do something?"

"'Course not, Zezé. At the most, she'll talk to the priest and the priest'll say, 'Best let it go, Maria. There's no messing with these people from the North.'"

He put the money in his pocket and rolled up his bag. Then, as always, he put his hand in his pocket and pulled out a folded brochure.

"This is for your sister Glória." He stretched. "It was a *helluva* good day!"

We rested for a moment.

"Ariovaldo."

"S'up?"

"What's a shooshy old witch?"

"How am I supposed to know, son? I made it up in the heat of the moment," he said with a chuckle.

"And were you really going to poke a hole in her?"

"'Course not. That was just to spook her."

"If you did poke a hole in her, would guts or straw come out?"

He laughed and ruffled my hair in a friendly manner.

"Know what, Zezé? I think shit would come out."

We both laughed.

"But don't be scared. I can't kill a thing. Not even a chicken. I'm so scared of the missus that I even let her beat me with the broomstick."

We stood and walked to the station. He shook my hand and said, "Just to be safe, we'll steer clear of that street for a few weeks."

He squeezed my hand even more tightly.

"See ya next week, champ."

I nodded while he slowly climbed the stairs.

From up top he shouted, "You're an angel, Zezé!"

I said good-bye and started to laugh.

Angel? If only he knew . . .

PART TWO

When the Baby Jesus
Appeared in All His Sadness

CHAPTER SIX

Piggybacks

"Chop-chop, Zezé, or you'll be late for school!"

I was sitting at the table, drinking a cup of coffee and chewing a piece of bread without any hurry. As always, I had my elbow on the table and was staring at the piece of paper on the wall.

Glória always got flustered. She couldn't wait for us to disappear for the morning and leave her in peace with the housework.

"Get a move on, you little rascal. You haven't

even combed your hair! You should follow Totoca's example — he's always ready on time."

She fetched a comb and ran it through my blond bangs.

"Not that there's anything to comb on this little goldilocks."

She made me stand and then looked me up and down to see if my shirt and trousers were decent.

"Now let's go, Zezé."

Totoca and I slung our satchels over our shoulders. Just textbooks, notebooks, and pencils inside. No snacks — they were for other children.

Glória patted the bottom of my satchel, felt the marbles, and smiled. We carried our tennis shoes in our hands to put on when we got to the market, near school.

The minute we were outside, Totoca would bolt off, leaving me to amble along on my own. That's when my inner imp would begin to wake up. I actually liked it when Totoca went on ahead so that I could do my thing in peace. I was fascinated with the highway. A piggyback. Definitely a piggyback. To cling to the back of a car and feel the highway blowing wind in your face, whooshing and whistling. It was the best thing in the world. We all did it. Totoca had taught me, telling me over and over to hold on tight, because the cars behind us were dangerous. We slowly learned to overcome our fear, and our sense of adventure prompted us to attempt even more difficult piggybacks. I was getting so bold that I'd even piggybacked on Seu Ladislau's car. The only one I hadn't been on was the Portuguese's beautiful vehicle. What a fine, well-kept car that was. The tires always brand-new. The metal so shiny you could see your reflection in it. I loved the sound of the horn: a gravelly moo, like a cow in a field. The Portuguese would drive past sitting stiffly in his seat, master of all that beauty, wearing the biggest scowl in the world. No one dared piggyback on his back wheel. They said he beat people up, killed them, and even threatened to cut off their balls before he killed them. None of the boys from school had dared to, until now.

When I talked about it earlier with Pinkie, he said, "No one at all, Zezé?"

"No one at all. They don't dare."

I sensed that Pinkie was laughing, and he could tell what I was thinking.

"But you're just dying to do it, aren't you?"

"To be honest, I am. I think . . ."

"What do you think?"

Now I was the one laughing.

"C'mon, tell me."

"You're so nosy."

"You always tell me — you always end up telling me. You can't help yourself."

"Hey, Pinkie. I leave home at seven o'clock in the morning, right? When I get to the corner, it's five past seven. Then, at ten past seven, the Portuguese stops his car at the corner outside the Misery and Hunger and goes in to buy a pack of cigarettes. . . . One of these days I'm going to pluck up the courage and wait for him to get back into the car and *pow*!"

"You don't dare."

"Don't I, Pinkie? I'll show you."

Now my heart was thumping. The car stopped; the Portuguese got out. Pinkie's challenge played on my fear and my courage; I didn't want to, but pride made me quicken my step. I walked around the bar and hid behind the corner, stuffing my shoes in my satchel while I was there. My heart was beating so fast, I was afraid they'd hear it in the bar. The Portuguese came back out without even noticing me. I heard the door open. . . .

"It's now or never, Pinkie!" I whispered.

I jumped onto the tire and clung to it with all my strength, fueled by my fear. I knew it was a long way to the school. I could already see the look on my classmates' faces when they learned of my prowess. . . .

"Aahh!"

I cried out so loudly that people raced to the door of the bar to see who had been run over.

I was suspended two feet above the ground, wriggling and writhing. My ears were burning like red-hot coals. My plan had gone wrong somehow. In my haste, I'd forgotten to listen for the engine to start.

The Portuguese's scowl looked even bigger than usual. His eyes were shooting sparks.

"Well, well, squirt. So, it's you, huh? You've got a lot of cheek for such a little fellow!"

He allowed my feet to touch the ground, let go

of one of my ears, and threatened me with his burly arm.

"Do you think I didn't see you checking out my car every day, squirt? I'm going to make sure you never try that again."

The humiliation hurt more than the physical pain. All I wanted to do was fire off a volley of swear words at the brute. But he wouldn't let go of me and, as if reading my mind, shook his free fist in my face and growled, "Say something then! Swear! Why don't you say anything?"

My eyes filled with tears; it was the pain, the humiliation, the sniggering onlookers.

The Portuguese carried on shouting.

"Why don't you swear at me, squirt?"

A cruel fury rose up in my chest, and I managed to splutter angrily, "I might not be saying anything, but I'm thinking it. And when I grow up, I'm going to kill you."

He laughed, followed by everyone standing around us.

"Well, grow up, then, squirt. I'll be waiting for you. But first I'm going to teach you a lesson."

He quickly let go of my ear and bent me over his thigh. He walloped me only once, but so hard it felt like he'd sent my backside through my stomach. Only then did he let me go.

I staggered away with the roar of the crowd ringing in my ears. It was only when I got to the other side of the highway, which I crossed without seeing a thing, that I was able to rub my stinging rump. The bastard! I'd show him. I swore I'd get even. I swore that . . . but the pain eased off as I put distance between myself and those sons of bitches. It'd be worse when the kids at school found out. And what was I going to tell Pinkie? For a week, whenever I passed the Misery and Hunger, they'd be laughing at me, in all their grown-up cowardice. I'd have to leave earlier and cross the highway farther down. . . .

I approached the market with these thoughts running through my mind. I washed my feet in the fountain and put on my shoes. Totoca was waiting for me anxiously. I wasn't going to breathe a word about my humiliation.

"Zezé, you've gotta help me."

"What've you done?"

"Remember Bié?"

"That big kid from Rua Barão de Capanema?"

"That's the one. He's going to get me at the gate after school. Can you fight him for me?"

"But he'll kill me."

"No, he won't and, anyway, you're brave and a good fighter."

"All right. At the gate?"

"At the gate."

Totoca always did that. He'd get in a fight, and then he'd have me sort it out. But it was a good thing. I would take out all my anger at the Portuguese on Bié.

But that day I took such a beating that I came out with a black eye and my arms all scratched up. Totoca knelt on the ground with the others, cheering me on, a pile of books on his knees: mine and his. He also shouted instructions.

"Head-butt him in the belly, Zezé. Bite him, dig in your nails—he's all lard. Kick him in the balls."

But even with all the cheering and instructions, if it weren't for Seu Rozemberg, Bié would have made mincemeat of me. He came out from behind the counter, grabbed Bié by the collar of his shirt, and knocked him around a bit.

"Have you no shame? A child your size beating up a little kid."

Everyone at home said that Seu Rozemberg had a secret crush on my sister Lalá. He knew us and whenever she was with us, he'd hand out pastries and sweets with the biggest of smiles dotted with several gold teeth.

I couldn't help myself and ended up telling Pinkie about my humiliation. I could hardly hide it with that puffy black eye. Besides, when Papa had seen me like that, he'd given me a few raps on the head and Totoca a dressing-down. Papa never hit Totoca, but he did me, because I was as bad as it got.

Pinkie must have heard every word, so how could I not tell him? He listened, indignant, and only when I finished did he say angrily, "What a coward!"

"The fight was nothing. You should have seen . . ."

Blow by blow, I relayed everything that had happened with the piggyback. Pinkie was amazed at how brave I'd been and said, "One day you'll get even."

"Yes, I will. I'm going to borrow Tom Mix's revolver and Fred Thomson's Silver King, and one day I'll bring him home in pieces."

But my anger quickly wore off, and soon we were talking about other things.

"Sweetie, guess what? Remember how last week I won that book *The Magic Rose* for being a good pupil?"

Pinkie liked it when I called him Sweetie; it let him know that I really loved him.

"Yes."

"Well, I've already read it. It's a story about a prince who is given a red and white rose by a fairy. The lucky fellow rides a handsome steed 'all festooned with gold'—that's what it says in the book. And on the steed all festooned with gold, he goes off in search of adventure. Whenever he's in danger, he shakes the magic rose and a big cloud of smoke appears so the prince can escape. To be honest, Pinkie, I think the story's a bit silly, you know? It's not like the adventures that I want to have in my life. Tom Mix and Buck Jones have real adventures. And Fred Thomson and Richard Talmadge. Because they

know how to fight, to shoot, to throw punches . . .
If they had to pull out a magic rose every time they
found themselves in danger, it'd be no fun at all.
What do you think?"

"Yeah, that'd be no fun."

"But that isn't what I want to know. I want to
know if you believe a rose can do magic like that."

"It does sound pretty weird."

"People tell stories and think children believe
everything."

"True."

We heard a noise. It was Luís coming over. My
little brother was becoming more and more beautiful. He wasn't a crybaby or the sort to throw tan-
trums. Even when I had to look after him, most of
the time I did so willingly.

I told Pinkie, "Let's change the subject, because
I'm going to tell him the story and he's going to
love it. You know that we shouldn't ruin a child's
illusions."

"Zezé, let's play?" said Luís.

"I'm already playing. What do you want to play?"

"I want to go to the zoo."

I looked at the chicken coop with the black hen and her two new chicks.

"It's too late. The lions are already asleep and the Bengal tigers too. It'll be closed by now. They won't let us in."

"Then let's travel around Europe."

The bright spark learned and repeated everything he heard perfectly. But, to be honest, I wasn't in the mood to travel around Europe either. What I really wanted was to hang out with Pinkie. Pinkie didn't tease me or make fun of my puffy eye.

I sat beside my little brother and spoke calmly.

"Just wait a second. I'll think of something for us to play."

Presently, the fairy of innocence flew past on a white cloud that ruffled the leaves on the trees, the grasses in the ditch, and Pinkie's leaves. A smile lit up my battered face.

"Was that you, Pinkie?"

"I didn't do anything."

"Oh, goody, then it's the windy season coming."

On our street there were all kinds of seasons. The marble season. The spinning-top season. The season to collect movie-star trading cards. The kite season was the most beautiful of them all. The skies would fill with kites of every color. Beautiful kites of every shape and size. It was war in the air. Headlong collisions, battles, lassoing, and line cutting.

Razors would cut strings, and kites would go wheeling through space, out of kilter, tangling bridles and tails; it was all beautiful. The world belonged to the kids in the street. In all the streets of Bangu. Then there'd be kite skeletons tangled in the electric wires, and we'd all run away from the power company truck. The men would come and angrily pull down the dead kites. The wind . . . the wind . . .

With the wind came the idea.

"Let's play hunting buffalo, Luís."

"I can't ride the horse."

"Soon you'll be big enough and you'll be able to. You sit there and watch how it's done."

Suddenly Pinkie became the most beautiful horse in the world, the wind blew stronger, and the scraggy grasses in the ditch became vast, lush plains. My cowboy outfit was festooned with gold. A sheriff's star flashed on my chest.

"Let's go, little horse, go. Run, run . . ."

Thubalup-thubalup-thubalup! I was back with Tom Mix and Fred Thomson. Buck Jones hadn't wanted to come this time, and Richard Talmadge was working on another film.

"Go, go, little horse. Run, run. Here come our Apache friends churning up dust as they ride."

Thubalup-thubalup-thubalup! The horses' hooves were making a racket.

"Run, run, little horse. The plains are full of bison and buffalo. Let's shoot, folks. *Bang, bang, bang! Pow, pow, pow!*"

Phwoo, phwoo, phwoo! whistled the arrows.

The wind, the speed, the wild gallop, the clouds of dust, and Luís's voice almost shouting.

"Zezé! Zezé!"

I slowly reined in my horse and jumped down, flushed from the ride.

"What's the matter? Did a buffalo come your way?"

"No. But let's play something else. I'm scared."

CHAPTER SEVEN

Making Friends

For the next few days, I left for school a little earlier to avoid running into the Portuguese buying cigarettes. I also took care to slip around the corner on the other side of the street, which was almost completely in the shade of the hedges in front of the houses. The minute I got to the highway, I would cross over and carry on, shoes in hand, staying close to the large factory wall. But my efforts were pointless. The street has a short memory, and soon no one remembered yet another of Seu Paulo's boy's antics. Because that's how I was known when I was being accused of something: "It was Seu Paulo's boy." "It was that boy of Seu Paulo's." "It was that little trouble-maker of Seu Paulo's." Once they even came up with a horrible joke: when the Bangu Football Club was thrashed by Andaraí, people joked, "Bangu took more of a beating than Seu Paulo's boy!"

Sometimes I'd see the goddamn car at the corner, and I'd hang back so as not to have to see the Portuguese—I really was going to kill him when I grew up—strutting his stuff as the owner of the most beautiful car in the world and in Bangu.

That was when he disappeared for a few days. What a relief! He must have gone out of town or taken a vacation. Once again I could walk to school with a calm heart, and I was already beginning to doubt whether it was really worth killing him later on. One thing was for sure: without fail, when I went for a piggyback on a less important car, I no longer felt the same thrill and my ears would begin to sting terribly.

Life in the street went on as always. Kite season had come, and we were always outside. The blue sky would be dotted with the most beautiful, colorful stars during the day. As it was the windy time of year, I didn't spend as much time with Pinkie, only going to see him when I was grounded, after a beating. I never tried to sneak out when I was grounded; being beaten twice in a row hurt a lot. Instead I would go with King Luís to festoon — I loved that word — my orange tree. As it happened, Pinkie had grown a lot and soon would be giving me flowers and fruit. Other orange trees took a long time. But my sweet orange tree was "precocious," which is how Uncle Edmundo described me. Then he told me what it meant: something that's ready a long time before everything else. Actually, I don't think he knew how to explain it properly. It just meant anything that came first.

So I'd fetch bits of rope and scraps of thread, make holes in a bunch of bottle tops, and go festoon Pinkie. You should have seen how smart he looked. When the wind blew, the bottle tops would clink against one another, and he looked like he was wearing the spurs Fred Thomson wore when he rode Silver King.

School life was good, too. I knew all the national anthems by heart. The big one was the real one. The others were the hymn to the flag and the one that went *"Liberty, Liberty, spread your wings over us."* For me, and I think for Tom Mix too, it was the best. Whenever we went for a ride, except when we were at war or on a hunt, he'd say respectfully, "C'mon, Apinajé warrior, sing the anthem of liberty."

My high-pitched voice would fill the vast plains, even more beautifully than when I sang with Seu Ariovaldo in my job as a singer's helper on Tuesdays.

Every Tuesday, I would skip school to wait for the train that brought my friend Ariovaldo. He'd come down the stairs holding up the brochures of song lyrics that we'd sell on the streets. He'd be carrying two more full bags too, which were our backup. He almost always sold everything, and this made both of us very happy.

At school recess, when there was time, we'd play marbles. I was really good at it. My aim was spot-on, and I almost never went home without my satchel jiggling with my winnings, often triple the number of marbles I'd gone with.

My teacher, Dona Cecília Paim, was really sweet. You could tell her I was the most terrible boy on my street, and she wouldn't believe it. She didn't believe that I knew more swear words than anyone else in class, or that no one got up to as much mischief as me. She refused to believe it. At school I was an angel. I was never told off and had become the darling of all the teachers, as I was one of the youngest kids who had ever been there. Dona Cecília Paim could see our poverty from a mile off and, at break time, when everyone else was eating their snack, she'd take pity on me, call me over, and send me off to buy a sweet pastry. She was so fond of me that I think I was good just so she wouldn't be disappointed with me.

Suddenly, it happened. I was walking along the highway slowly, as always, when the Portuguese's car drove past, very close. He honked the horn three times, and I saw that the monster was smiling at me. All over again I felt angry and wanted to kill him when I grew up. I scowled haughtily and pretended to ignore him.

* * *

"It's like I said, Pinkie. Every single day. It's as if he waits for me to go past, and then he comes along and beeps his horn three times. Yesterday he even waved."

"What did you do?"

"I don't care. I pretend not to see him. He's starting to get scared, you see. I'll be six soon, and it won't be long before I'm a man."

"Do you think he wants to be your friend because he's scared?"

"I'm sure of it. Wait a second, I'm going to get the crate."

Pinkie had grown a lot. I had to stand on a crate to climb into his saddle now.

"There, now we can talk properly."

Up high there I felt bigger than everything. I'd look around at the landscape, at the grass in the ditch, at the tanagers and finches that came to look for food. At night, darkness would barely have fallen when another Luciano would come swooping happily around my head like a plane at the Campo dos Afonsos air base. At first even Pinkie was surprised that I wasn't afraid, because most children are terrified of bats. Come to think of it, Luciano hadn't appeared for days. He must have found other Campo dos Afonsos air bases to fly around.

"Did you know, Pinkie, the guavas at Eugênia's house are starting to turn yellow. They must be just about ripe. The problem is if she catches me. I've already been beaten three times today. I'm here because I'm grounded. . . ."

But the devil gave me a hand down and pulled me over to the hedge. The afternoon breeze was starting to waft the smell of the guavas to my nose, so it seemed. I peered through the hedge, pushed a branch aside, heard no noise . . . And the devil was saying, "Go on, silly, can't you see there's no one there? She must have gone to the Japanese lady's grocery store. Seu Benedito? Don't worry. He's practically blind and deaf. He can't see a thing. There's time to run away if he notices."

I followed the hedge to the ditch and decided. First, I signaled to Pinkie to be quiet. By now my heart was racing. There was no messing with Eugênia. God knows she had a tongue on her.

I was tiptoeing along, holding my breath, when her voice boomed from the kitchen window.

"What's going on, boy?"

It didn't even occur to me to lie and say I'd come to fetch a ball. I bolted and jumped into the ditch with a splash. But something else was waiting for me there. A pain so intense that I almost screamed, but if I screamed I'd get beaten twice: first, because I'd left the backyard when I was grounded and, second, because I'd been stealing guavas from the neighbor and had just managed to get a shard of glass in my left foot.

Still giddy with pain, I tugged at the glass. I moaned quietly and saw the blood swirling into the dirty water in the ditch. What now? My eyes brimming with tears, I managed to remove the glass, but I had no idea how to stanch the flow of blood. I was squeezing my ankle hard to ease the pain. I had to stay strong. Night had almost fallen, and with it, Papa, Mama, and Lalá would arrive home. If any of them caught me, they'd beat me. Or they'd each beat me separately. I climbed over the barrier and hopped over to my orange tree, where I sat down. It still hurt a lot, but I didn't feel like I was going to be sick anymore.

"Look, Pinkie."

Pinkie was horrified. He was like me — he didn't like the sight of blood.

Oh Lord, what was I going to do?

Totoca would have helped me, but where was he now? There was Glória. She was in the kitchen, no doubt. Glória was the only one who didn't like the fact that everyone was always beating me. She might give my ears a tug or ground me again. But I had to try.

I dragged myself to the kitchen door, trying to think of a way to win Glória's sympathy. She was embroidering something. I sat down awkwardly, and this time God helped me. She looked over and saw me with my head down. She didn't say anything because I was grounded. My eyes welled up with tears and I sniffed. I found her eyes on me again. She had stopped embroidering.

"What is it, Zezé?"

"Nothing, Gló . . . Why doesn't anyone love me?"

"You get up to a lot of mischief."

"I've been beaten three times today, Gló."

"And didn't you deserve it?"

"That's not it. It's just that because no one loves me, they take everything out on me."

Glória's fifteen-year-old heart was beginning to thaw, and I could feel it.

"I think it's best if a car runs over me on the highway tomorrow and squashes me completely."

Then the tears came streaming down in torrents.

"Nonsense, Zezé. I love you lots."

"No, you don't. If you did, you wouldn't let them beat me again today."

"It's getting dark now, and there won't be enough time for you to get in trouble again."

"But I already have. . . ."

She put down her embroidery and came over. She almost screamed when she saw the puddle of blood at my foot.

"My God! Shrimp, what've you done?"

I'd won. If she called me shrimp, I was safe.

She picked me up and sat me down on the chair. Then she quickly got a bowl of salty water and knelt at my feet.

"This is going to hurt a lot, Zezé."

"It's already hurting a lot."

"My God, the cut's almost an inch and a half long. How did you do it?"

"Don't tell anyone. Please, Gló, I promise to be good. Don't let them hit me so much. . . ."

"OK, I won't tell. But what are we going to do? Everyone's going to see your foot all bandaged up. And tomorrow you won't be able to go to school. They're going to find out."

"I'll go to school. I'll wear my shoes to the corner. After that I can take them off."

"You need to lie down and put your foot up. Otherwise you won't even be able to walk tomorrow."

She helped me limp over to my bed.

"I'll bring you something to eat before the others get home."

When she came back with the food, I couldn't help myself and gave her a kiss. I hardly ever did that.

When everyone had assembled for dinner, Mama noticed that I was missing.

"Where's Zezé?"

"He's lying down. He's been complaining of a headache all day."

I listened in ecstasy, momentarily forgetting how much my foot hurt. I liked being the topic of conversation. That was when Glória decided to stick up for me. She put on a voice that was sorrowful and accusatory at the same time.

"I think everyone's been hitting him. And today he was in really bad shape. Three beatings is too much."

"But he's always up to no good. He only stops when he gets a paddling! Do you mean to say you never lay a finger on him?"

"Hardly ever. At the most, I give his ears a tug."

They all fell silent and Glória went on.

"After all, he isn't even six yet. Yes, he's naughty, but he's still a child."

That conversation pleased me no end.

Glória was fretting as she got me dressed, helping me to put on my shoes.

"Are you OK to go?"

"I'll be fine."

"You're not going to do something silly on the highway, are you?"

"Nope."

"Was it true what you said?"

"No. It's just that I was really sad 'cause I thought no one loved me."

She ran her hands over my fine blond hair and sent me off.

I thought it would only be hard until I got to the highway and that once I took off my shoes, the pain would ease up. But when my bare foot touched the ground, it was too much and I had to go slowly, leaning against the wall of the factory. At that rate I'd never get there.

Then the thing happened. The horn honked three times. Damn! It wasn't enough that I was dying of pain and here he was to bully me.

The car pulled up alongside me. He stuck his body out and called, "Hey, squirt, you hurt your foot?"

I felt like saying that it was none of his business. But because he hadn't called me anything worse than squirt, I didn't reply and kept walking.

He started the car again, passed me, and pulled over to the side of the road, blocking me. He opened the door and got out, his large body towering over mine.

"Is it hurting a lot, squirt?"

It wasn't possible that a person who had beaten me was now speaking in such a gentle, almost friendly, voice. He came even closer and, unexpectedly, knelt down and looked me in the eye. His smile was so soft it seemed to radiate affection.

"It looks like you've really hurt yourself. What happened?"

I sniffed a little before replying.

"Piece of glass."

"Is it deep?"

I showed him with my fingers.

"Oh! That's serious. Why didn't you stay home? You're on your way to school, aren't you?"

"My parents don't know I hurt myself. If they find out, they'll beat me to teach me not to get hurt."

"Come with me. I'll take you."

"No, thank you, sir."

"Why not?"

"Everyone at school knows what happened that time."

"But you can't walk like that."

It was true. I hung my head, feeling that my pride was about to take a tumble.

He lifted my head up by the chin.

"Let's forget a few things. Ever been in a car?"

"No, sir, never."

"Then I'm going to give you a lift."

"I can't. We're enemies."

"I don't care. If you're ashamed, I'll drop you off before we get to the school. OK?"

I was so moved I didn't even reply. I just nodded. He picked me up, opened the door, and sat me carefully in the passenger seat. He walked around the car and got in. Before starting the engine, he smiled at me again.

"That's better, see?"

The lovely feeling of the car cruising along, with the occasional jiggle, made me close my eyes and begin to dream. It was smoother and nicer than Fred Thomson's horse, Silver King. But it wasn't for long because when I opened my eyes, we were almost at the school. I could already see the crowd of schoolchildren swarming through the front gate. Terrified,

I slid off the seat and hid. I said angrily, "You promised to stop before we got to the school."

"I changed my mind. That foot of yours can't be left like that. You could get tetanus."

I couldn't even ask what that beautiful, tricky word was. I also knew it was pointless saying I didn't want to go. The car turned onto Rua das Casinhas, and I returned to the seat.

"You strike me as a brave little man. Let's go see if it's true."

He pulled up in front of the pharmacy and carried me inside in his arms. When Dr. Adaucto Luz came to help us, I was terrified. He was doctor to the factory staff and knew Papa well. And my fear grew bigger when he me looked at me and asked straight off the bat, "You're Paulo Vasconcelos's son, aren't you? Has he found a position yet?"

I had to answer, although I was ashamed that the Portuguese now knew that Papa was unemployed.

"He's waiting. He's been promised a lot of things. . . ."

"Well, let's get down to business."

He peeled back the cloth stuck to the cut and let

out an "Uh-oh" that frightened me. My lips began to quiver. But the Portuguese came to my rescue.

They sat me on a table covered with white sheets. A bunch of tools appeared. And I shook. The only reason I didn't shake more was because the Portuguese leaned my back against his chest and held me by the shoulders, firmly but gently.

"It won't hurt much. When it's over, I'll take you for a soda and sweets. If you don't cry, I'll buy you some sweets that come with trading cards."

I mustered up all the courage I could. The tears streamed down my face, and I let them do everything. They gave me stitches and even an anti-tetanus injection. I struggled against the desire to throw up. The Portuguese held me tight as if he wanted to take on a little of my pain. He mopped my sweaty hair and face with his handkerchief. It felt like it was never going to end. But it did eventually.

When he took me to the car, he was satisfied. He had done everything he'd promised. Except that now I didn't want anything. It was as if my soul had been torn out through my feet.

"You can't go to school now, squirt."

We were in the car and I was sitting very close to him, leaning against his arm, almost getting in the way of his driving.

"I'll take you somewhere near your house. You make something up. You can say you got hurt at play-time and that the teacher sent you to the pharmacy."

I looked at him with appreciation.

"You're a brave little man, squirt."

I smiled through the pain, but inside that pain I had just discovered something important. The Portuguese was now the person I liked most in the world.

CHAPTER EIGHT

Conversations, Here and There

"Hey, Pinkie, I already know practically everything. Everything. He lives on Rua Barão de Capanema. Right at the end. He parks his car next to his house. He has two cages, one with a canary in it and another with a bluebird in it. I went there really early with my shoe-shine box, acting all casual. I wanted to go so badly, Pinkie, that the box didn't even feel heavy this time. I had a good look at the house and thought it was too big for a person to live in alone. He was down the side, at the washtub. Shaving.

"I clapped my hands.

"'Want your shoes shined, sir?'

"He came out to the front with his face covered in soap, one bit already shaved. He smiled and said, 'Oh, it's you! Come in, squirt.'

"I followed him.

"'Just wait—I'll be done in a minute.'

"And he scraped his face with the razor: *kechah, kechah, kechah. When I'm all grown-up,* I thought, *I want stubble that sounds like that when I shave: kechah, kechah, kechah . . .*

"I sat on my box and waited. He looked at me in the mirror.

"'Aren't you supposed to be in school?'

"'Today's a public holiday, sir. That's why I'm out shining shoes, to make a few tostões.'

"'I see.'

"And he went back to shaving. Then he leaned over the washtub, splashed water on his face, and dried it with a towel. His face looked flushed and shiny. He laughed again.

"'Want to have breakfast with me?'

"I said I didn't, even though I did.

"'Come on in.'

"You should have seen how clean and neat it was. He had a red-checkered tablecloth and even proper coffee cups. Not tin cups like the ones at home. He said an old black woman came every day to tidy up when he went to work.

"'If you like, dunk your bread in the coffee like this. But don't slurp when you take a sip. It's bad manners.'"

I looked at Pinkie, but he was as quiet as a rag doll.

"What?"

"Nothing. I'm listening."

"Look, Pinkie, I don't like arguments, but if you're upset, you'd best say so now."

"It's just that all you do now is play with the Portuguese, and I can't join in."

I thought about it. Of course. It hadn't even occurred to me that he couldn't join in.

"In a couple of days we're going to meet Buck Jones. I sent him a message through Chief Sitting Bull. Buck Jones is far away, hunting in the savanna. And Pinkie, is it savanna or savanna? I'm not sure.

Next time I go to Gran's, I'll ask Uncle Edmundo."

Silence again.

"Now, where were we?"

"Dunking coffee in bread."

I laughed.

"You don't dunk coffee in bread, silly."

"Anyway, me and the Portuguese were both quiet and he just looked at me, studying me.

"'So you managed to find out where I live.'

"I felt uncomfortable and decided to come clean.

"'Promise not to get mad if I tell you something, sir?'

"'Of course. There should be no secrets between friends.'

"'I haven't shined any shoes today.'

"'I suspected that was the case.'

"'But I really wanted to . . . Over this side no one needs their shoes dusted off. It's only people who live near the highway.'

"'But you could have come without lugging all that weight around, no?'

"'If I didn't lug all this weight around, I wouldn't

have been allowed out. I can't wander off very far. Every now and then, I have to show my face at home, you see? To go farther away, I have to pretend I'm working.'

"He laughed at my logic.

"'If I'm working, they know I'm not getting up to mischief. It's better this way, because I don't get beaten as much.'

"'I don't believe you're as naughty as you say you are.'

"Then I went really serious.

"'I'm worthless, really bad. That's why it's the devil that's born in my heart on Christmas Day, not Baby Jesus, and I never get a single present. I'm a pest, sir. A nuisance. A dog. A lowlife. One of my sisters said that a wretch like me shouldn't have been born.'

"He scratched his head in surprise.

"'Just this week I've had several beatings. Some of them hurt a lot. I also get beaten for things I didn't do. I get blamed for everything. Everyone hits me.'

"'But what do you do that's so bad?'

"'It really must be the devil's work. I get this itch

to do something, and then I do it. This week I set fire to Eugênia's fence. I called Dona Cordélia a hippo, and she got really mad. I kicked a ball of rags, and the stupid thing went through Dona Narcisa's window and broke her big mirror. I broke three streetlights with my slingshot. I hit Seu Abel's son with a stone.'

"'Enough, enough.'

"He covered his mouth with his hand to hide his smile.

"'But there's more. I pulled up all the seedlings that Dona Tentena had just planted. I made Dona Rosena's cat swallow a marble.'

"'Oh! That's no good. I don't like to see animals mistreated.'

"'It wasn't a big one. It was really tiny. They gave the critter a laxative and it came out. Instead of giving me back my marble, they gave me a thrashing. Or worse, one time I was asleep and Papa took his sandal and whacked me. I didn't even know why he was hitting me.'

"'And why was it?'

"'A whole bunch of us had gone to the cinema.

We'd gone on a Monday 'cause it's cheaper. And when we were there, I needed to go, you know? So I stood in the corner by the wall and went. And it went trickling down. It's silly to leave and miss part of the film. But you know what boys are like, sir. If one does something, then everyone else wants to do it, too. So they all took turns in the corner, and the trickle turned into a river. They ended up finding out, and you know what they said: "It was Seu Paulo's boy." So they banned me from the Cinema Bangu for a year, until I learned how to behave. That night the owner told Papa, and he wasn't impressed, believe me.'"

Pinkie was still pouting.

"Look, Pinkie, you don't need to be like this. He's my best friend. But you're the absolute king of the trees, just like Luís is the absolute king of my brothers. Our hearts need to be big enough for everything we love, you know."

Silence.

"Know what, Pinkie? I'm going to play marbles. You're very grumpy lately."

* * *

In the beginning it was only a secret because I was afraid to be seen in the car of the man who had walloped me. Afterward I kept it up because it was nice to have a secret. And the Portuguese went along with it. We had made a pact that no one would ever find out about our friendship. First, because he didn't want to give lifts to all the kids. When we saw people we knew, or even Totoca, I would slide down in the seat. Second, because we didn't want anyone interrupting us, as we had lots to talk about.

"Have you ever seen my mother, sir? She's an Apinajé Indian. Her parents were real Indians. We're all half Indians."

"So how did you turn out so fair? With this almost white-blond hair, to boot?"

"It's the Portuguese side of the family. Mama looks like an Indian. She's really dark with straight hair. Only Glória and I came out fair. Mama works on the looms at the English Mill to help pay the bills. The other day she went to load a box of spools, and suddenly she felt this sharp pain. She had to go to the doctor. He gave her a girdle to wear 'cause of a hernia in her back. Mama's quite nice to me. When she smacks me, she gets a switch of arrowleaf from the backyard and only hits me on the legs. She's always so tired when she gets home at night that she doesn't even feel like talking."

The car cruised and I chattered.

"My oldest sister's really something. She's such a flirt. When Mama used to ask her to look after us and take us for a walk, she'd tell her not to go up to the top of the street because she knew she had a boyfriend waiting at the corner. So she'd head down to the bottom of the street, and there'd be another boyfriend waiting there. You couldn't leave any pencils around, 'cause she was always writing letters to her boyfriends. . . ."

"Here we are."

We were near the market, and he was pulling over at the place we'd agreed on.

"See you tomorrow, squirt."

He knew I'd find a way to get him to stop off with me for a soda and a few trading cards. I'd already figured out the times when he didn't have much to do.

It had been going on for more than a month. Much more. But I never knew an adult could look as sad as he did when I told him the stories about Christmas. His eyes filled with tears and he stroked my head, promising that I would never go without a Christmas present again.

The days passed slowly and, above all, happily. People were beginning to notice my transformation, even at home. I wasn't getting up to as much mischief and was always off in my own little world in the backyard. It's true that sometimes the devil got the better of me. But I didn't swear as much as I used to, and I left the neighbors in peace.

Whenever he could, the Portuguese would invent an outing, and it was on one of these outings that he pulled the car over and smiled at me.

"Do you like riding in 'our' car?"

"Is it mine too?"

"Everything that's mine is yours. Like two really good friends."

I was ecstatic. If only I could tell everyone that I was half owner of the most beautiful car in the world.

"So, does this mean that now we're completely friends?" he asked.

"Yes."

"Then can I ask you something?"

"Yes, sir."

"You don't want to grow up quickly so you can kill me anymore, do you?"

"No. I'd never do that."

"But you said it, didn't you?"

"I said it when I was angry. I'm never going to kill anyone because when they kill chickens at home, I can't even watch. Then I discovered that you're not what they say you are. You're not a cannibal or anything."

He almost jumped.

"What did you say?"

"Cannibal."

"And do you know what that is?"

"Yes, I do, sir. Uncle Edmundo taught me. He's a wise man. There's a man in the city who invited him to make a dictionary. The only thing he's never been able to explain to me is what a carborundum is."

"You're changing the subject. I want you to explain to me what a cannibal is, exactly."

"Cannibals used to eat human flesh. In the history book, there's a picture of one skinning some Portuguese because he's going to eat them. They also ate warriors from enemy tribes."

He gave a sort of belly laugh that I'd never heard from a Brazilian.

"You're priceless, squirt. You make my jaw drop sometimes."

Then he gave me a serious look.

"Tell me, squirt, how old are you?"

"My pretend age or my real one?"

"Real, of course. I don't want a friend who lies."

"It's like this: I'm really five. But I pretend I'm six; otherwise they won't let me go to school."

"And why did they put you in school so early?"

"Ha! Everyone wanted me out of their hair for a few hours. Do you know what carborundum is?"

"Where'd you get that from?"

I put my hand in my pocket and felt around among the pebbles, slingshot, trading cards, spinning-top string, and marbles.

"It's this."

I held up a medallion with a picture of a head on it. A North American Indian, with feathers in his hair. The word was written on the back.

He turned the medallion over in his hand.

"I'm afraid I don't know either. Where did you find this?"

"It's part of Papa's pocket watch. It had a strap with this on the end, which was supposed to hang out of his pocket. Papa said the watch was going to be my inheritance. But then he needed money and had to sell it. Such a beautiful watch. He gave me the rest of the inheritance, which was this. I cut off the strap because it smelled funny."

He stroked my hair again.

"You're a complicated little chap, but I have to confess you're filling this old heart with joy. Indeed you are. Shall we go now?"

"This is so nice. Just a little more. I need to say something very serious, sir."

"Go ahead."

"So, we're really friends, right?"

"Absolutely."

"Even the car is half mine, isn't it?"

"One day it will be yours, all of it."

"It's just that . . ."

It was hard to get out.

"Go on. . . . What's the matter? You're not one to get tongue-tied. . . ."

"You won't get angry?"

"'Course not."

"There are two things I don't like about our friendship."

But it didn't come out as easily as I had planned.

"What are they?"

"First, if we're such good friends, then why should I have to call you 'sir' or 'Seu Manuel' all the time?"

He laughed.

"You can call me whatever you want."

"It's just that I don't know what to call you when I talk to Pinkie about you. You're not upset?"

"Why would I be? It's a fair request. Who's this Pinkie that I've never heard of?"

"Pinkie is Sweetie."

"So, Sweetie is Pinkie and Pinkie is Sweetie. I'm still lost."

"Pinkie is my little orange tree. And Sweetie is my nickname for him."

"So, you have a little orange tree named Pinkie."

"He's incredible. He talks to me, turns into a horse, comes on adventures with us. With Buck Jones, Tom Mix . . . Fred Thomson . . . Do you like Ken Maynard?" (It was odd leaving off the "sir," but I'd made up my mind.)

He made a gesture as if to say he didn't know anything about cowboys in Westerns.

"The other day Fred Thomson introduced me to him. I really like the leather hat he wears. But I don't think he knows how to laugh."

"Well, let's get a move on, because the world in that little head of yours is confusing me. What's the other thing?"

"The other thing's even more difficult. But since I brought up the 'sir' and you didn't get upset. . . . I don't like your name very much. It's not that I don't like it, but among friends it's a bit . . ."

"Goodness me, what now?"

"Do you really think I can call you Valadares?"

He thought about it a little and smiled.

"No, it doesn't sound right."

"I don't like Manuel either. You've no idea how angry I get when Papa tells Portuguese jokes and says, 'Manuel this, Manuel that.' You can tell that the son of a gun's never had a Portuguese friend. . . ."

"What did you just say?"

"That Papa tells Portuguese jokes?"

"No. After that. Something rude."

"Is 'son of a gun' as bad as 'son of a bitch'?"

"It's almost the same."

"Then I'll try not to say it. . . . So, what do you think?"

"You tell me. Have you got a solution? You don't want to call me Valadares, and by the sound of things, Manuel won't do either."

"There's one name I love."

"What?"

I made the cheekiest face in the world.

"What Seu Ladislau and the others call you at the pastry shop."

He shook his fist, pretending to be angry.

"Why, you're the cockiest person I know. You want to call me 'Portuga,' don't you?"

"It's a good name for a friend."

"Is that all you want? Very well, then. Shall we go now?"

He started the engine and drove a distance, thinking. Then he stuck his head out the window and looked up and down the street. No one was coming.

He opened the car door and said, "Out."

I obeyed and followed him to the back of the car. He pointed at the spare tire.

"Now, hold on tight. And be careful."

I positioned myself for the piggyback, happy as could be. He climbed into the car and drove off slowly. He stopped after five minutes and came to check on me.

"Like it?"

"It's like a dream."

"Well, that's enough. Let's go—it's getting late."

Night was gently falling and off in the distance crickets were singing in the hawthorn trees, announcing that there was more summer to come.

The car purred along.

"Well. From now on, we'll leave that subject well alone. OK?"

"Done."

"I'd like to see you explaining where you've been all this time when you get home."

"I've already got it worked out. I'm going to say I went to Catechism. Today's Thursday, isn't it?"

"You're incorrigible. You've got an excuse for everything."

I scooted over close to him and leaned my head on his arm.

"Portuga!"

"What?"

"I never want to be far away from you, you know?"

"Why is that?"

"Because you're the best person in the world. No one treats me badly when I'm with you, and I feel a sun of happiness in my heart."

CHAPTER NINE

Two Memorable Beatings

"You folded it here. Now, take the knife and cut the paper right on the fold."

The dull sound of the edge of the knife cutting the paper.

"Now, glue it on, overlapping just a tiny bit, leaving this much margin. Like this."

I was sitting next to Totoca, learning to make a balloon. After everything was glued down, Totoca pegged it on the clothesline by the crown.

"You only make the mouth when it's all dry. Got it, dummy?"

"Yep."

We sat there on the back doorstep staring at the colorful balloon, which was taking a long time to dry. Totoca, as self-appointed expert, went on explaining, "You should only try to make a balloon with lots of sections when you've really got the hang of it. In the beginning you should just make them with two, 'cause it's easier."

"Totoca, if I make a balloon on my own, will you make the mouth for me?"

"That depends."

This was him trying to cut a deal, to take a crack at my marble or trading card collections, which were growing faster than anyone could understand.

"Gee, Totoca, I fight for you when you ask me to."

"OK. I'll do the first one for free, but if you don't learn, the others'll only be in exchange for something."

"Fine."

I swore to myself that I was going to learn so well that he'd never touch my balloons again.

After that I couldn't get the balloon out of my head. It had to be "my" balloon. Imagine how proud Portuga would be when he heard of my prowess. Pinkie's admiration when he saw the thing swinging from my hand . . .

The idea had taken hold of me, so I filled my pockets with marbles and a few trading cards that I had repeats of and headed out. I would sell them on the cheap in order to buy at least two sheets of tissue paper.

"Attention, everyone! Five marbles for one tostão. Good as new!"

Nothing happened.

"Ten cards for one tostão. You won't find them as cheap at Dona Lota's shop."

Nothing happened. None of the children had any money. I went all the way down Rua do Progresso peddling my wares. I visited Rua Barão de Capanema almost at a trot, but nothing happened. What about Gran's house? I went there too, but she wasn't interested.

"I don't want trading cards or marbles. You're better off hanging on to them. Because tomorrow you'll come and ask me to buy them for you again."

Gran obviously didn't have any money.

I headed off again and looked down at my legs. They were dirty from so much walking through dusty streets. I looked at the sun, which was beginning to set. That was when the miracle happened.

"Zezé! Zezé!"

Biriquinho came running like a madman down the street toward me.

"I've been looking everywhere for you. Are you selling?"

I shook my pockets, jiggling the marbles.

"Let's sit down."

We sat and I spread my wares on the ground.

"How much?"

"Five marbles for one tostão and ten cards for the same price."

"That's steep."

He annoyed me with that. What a thief! How was it "steep" when everyone sold five cards and three marbles for what I was asking? I went to put them all back in my pocket.

"Wait. Can I pick which ones?"

"How much you got?"

"Three tostões. I can spend two."

"OK, then, I can give you six marbles and twelve cards."

I raced into the Misery and Hunger. No one remembered *that scene* anymore. Only Seu Orlando was there, chatting at the counter. When the factory siren sounded, everyone came to wet their throats and you couldn't even get inside.

"Have you got any tissue paper, sir?"

"You got money? You're not putting anything else on your father's tab."

I wasn't offended. I just showed him the two tostões.

"I've only got pink and orange."

"Is that all?"

"You lot made off with everything I had during the kite season. But what difference does it make? Kites fly no matter what the color, don't they?"

"But it's not for a kite. I'm going to make my first balloon. I want my first balloon to be the most beautiful one in the world."

There was no time to lose. It would take ages to get to Chico Franco's general store.

"I'll take it."

Now things were going to be different. I put a chair next to the table and helped King Luís up so he could watch.

"Now, you be quiet, all right? Zezé is going to do something very tricky. When you grow up, I'll teach you how to do it for free."

It was growing dark quickly, and there we were working. The factory siren sounded. I needed to be quick. Jandira was already putting the plates on the table. She liked to feed us first so we didn't disturb the grown-ups.

"Zezé! Luís!"

She bellowed as if we were all the way over in Murundu. I helped Luís down and said, "You go. I'll be right behind you."

"Zezé! Get a move on, or there'll be trouble."

"Coming!"

The witch was in a bad mood. She must have had a fight with one of her boyfriends. The one down at the bottom of the street or the one up at the top.

Now, almost as if on purpose, the glue was drying and the flour was sticking to my fingers, making it hard to work.

Her bellow was even louder. There was barely any light to work by.

"Zezé!"

It was the last straw. Jandira was furious.

"You think I'm your servant? Come eat now!"

She rushed into the living room, grabbed me by the ears, dragged me into the kitchen, and threw me against the table. That made me mad.

"I won't eat. I won't. I won't. I want to finish my balloon."

I slipped away and raced back to where I'd been.

She turned into a beast. Instead of coming at me, she went to the table and that was the end of my balloon. She tore it to shreds. I was so shocked, I did nothing. Then, not satisfied, she grabbed me by the arms and legs and threw me into the middle of the room.

"When I tell you to do something, you obey me."

The devil inside me worked its way free. My indignation exploded like a hurricane. The first blast was simple.

"Do you know what you are? You're a whore!"

She put her face close to mine, her eyes shooting sparks.

"Say that again if you've got the guts."

I dragged the word out.

"Whooore!"

She snatched up the leather strap from the chest of drawers and began to flog me mercilessly. I turned my back to her and hid my head in my hands. My fury was greater than the pain.

"Whore! Whore! Bitch!"

She didn't stop. My body was burning up with pain. That was when Totoca came in and ran to help her, as she was beginning to tire.

"Go ahead and kill me, you murderer! You'll get what you deserve in prison!"

And she went on flogging me, hitting me so hard I fell to my knees, leaning on the chest of drawers.

"Whore! Bitch."

Totoca picked me up and turned me around.

"Cut it out, Zezé. You can't talk to your sister like that."

"She's a whore. A murderer. A bitch!"

Then he started to hit me in the face — the eyes, the nose, and the mouth. Especially the mouth.

My salvation was that Glória heard. She was next door chatting with Dona Rosena and rushed back home when she heard all the shouting. She blew into the living room like a gale. There was no messing with Glória, and when she saw my face covered in blood, she pushed Totoca aside and shoved Jandira away too, not caring that she was the oldest. I was sprawled on the ground, almost unable to open my eyes, taking ragged breaths. She took me to the bedroom. I didn't cry, but King Luís had gone to hide in Mama's room and was bawling, terrified, because they were hurting me.

Glória was ranting.

"One day you're going to kill this child and then what, you heartless monsters?"

She had laid me down on the bed and was going to fetch the blessed bowl of salty water. Totoca came in awkwardly. Glória gave him a shove.

"Get lost, you coward!"

"Didn't you hear what he was calling Jandira?"

"He wasn't doing anything. You two provoked him. When I left, he was quietly making his balloon. You have no heart. How can you beat your brother so badly?"

As she was wiping the blood off me, I spat a piece of tooth into the bowl. That stoked the volcano.

"Look what you've done, you lily liver. When you want to fight, you get scared and go running to him for help. Chicken! Nine years old and you still wet the bed. I'm going to show everyone your mattress and the wet pajamas you hide in the drawer every morning."

Then she sent everyone out of the room and locked the door. She turned on the light because night had fallen. She took off my shirt and sat there mopping the blood and gashes on my body.

"Does it hurt, shrimp?"

"It's hurting a lot now."

"I'll do it really softly, my sweet little rascal. You'll need to lie on your stomach for a while so it can dry; otherwise your clothes'll stick to the cuts and it'll hurt."

But what really hurt was my face. It ached with pain and rage at so much unprovoked cruelty.

When things were a little better, she lay down beside me, stroking my head.

"You saw, Gló. I wasn't doing anything. When I deserve it, I don't mind being flogged. But I wasn't doing anything."

She gulped.

"But the saddest part was my balloon. It was looking so beautiful. Just ask Luís."

"I believe you. It was beautiful. But don't worry. Tomorrow we'll go to Gran's house and buy some tissue paper. And I'll help you make the most beautiful balloon in the world. So beautiful that even the stars will be jealous."

"There's no point, Gló. You only make one beautiful first balloon. When that one doesn't work out, you never get it right again or you never feel like making it again."

"One day . . . one day . . . I'm going to take you

far away from this house. We're going to live . . ."

She stopped short. She must have been thinking about Gran's house, but it would be the same hell there. That was when she decided to enter the world of the orange tree and my dreams.

"I'm going to take you to live on Tom Mix's or Buck Jones's ranch."

"But I like Fred Thomson even better."

"Then let's go there."

And, completely helpless, we began to weep quietly together. . . .

Even though I missed Portuga, I didn't go to see him for two days. I wasn't even allowed to go to school. They didn't want there to be any witnesses to such brutality. As soon as the swelling on my face went down and my lips healed, I would go back to my normal routine. I spent the days sitting next to Pinkie with my little brother, with no desire to talk. Afraid of everything. Papa had sworn that he'd beat me to a pulp if I ever repeated what I'd said to Jandira again. Now I was even afraid to breathe. Best to take refuge in the tiny shadow of my orange tree, look through the mountains of trading cards that Portuga had given me, and patiently teach King Luís to play marbles. He was a bit clumsy, but he'd eventually get the hang of it.

I missed Portuga a lot. He must have thought it odd that I hadn't been to see him, and if he'd known where I lived, he might even have come looking for me. My ears sorely missed his thick Portuguese accent and the way he always called me tu. Dona Cecília Paim had told me that you really need to know your grammar to address others as tu. My eyes longed to see his brown face, his impeccable dark-colored clothes, the collars of his shirts, always so stiff, as if they'd come straight out of a drawer, his checkered waistcoat, and even his gold anchor cuff links.

But I'd be better soon. Children heal quickly, or so they say. That night Papa hadn't gone out. No one else was home, except for Luís, who was already asleep. Mama was probably on her way home from the city. Sometimes she did overtime at the English Mill, and we only saw her on Sundays.

I had decided to stay near Papa, because that way I couldn't get up to any mischief. He was sitting in the rocking chair staring blankly at the wall. His face was always covered in stubble. His shirt wasn't always terribly clean. Maybe he hadn't gone to play cards with his friends because he had no money. Poor Papa — it must have made him sad that Mama had to work to help pay the bills. Lalá already had a job at the factory. It must have been hard to go looking for jobs and always come home downcast after hearing the same reply: "We need someone younger."

Sitting on the doorstep, I was counting little white geckos on the wall and glancing at Papa from time to time. The only other time I'd seen him looking so sad was that Christmas morning. I needed to do something for him. Maybe I could sing for him. I could sing very softly and for sure it would cheer him up a little. I went through my repertoire in my head and remembered the last song Seu Ariovaldo had taught me. "The Tango"; the tango was one of the most beautiful things I'd ever heard. I started softly:

> "*I want a naked woman tonight*
> *Very naked I want her to be . . .*
> *I want her in the full-moon light*

I want her body all to me . . ."

"Zezé!"

"Yes, Papa?"

I stood up quickly. Papa must have liked it a lot and wanted me to sing it closer to him.

"What's that you're singing?"

I repeated it.

"I want a naked woman tonight . . ."

"Who taught you that song?"

His eyes had taken on a dull shine as if he was about to go crazy.

"Seu Ariovaldo."

"I already told you I don't want you anywhere near him."

He hadn't said any such thing. I don't even think he knew I worked as a singer's helper.

"Sing it again."

"It's a popular tango."

"I want a naked woman tonight . . ."

A slap exploded on my face.

"Sing it again."

"I want a naked woman tonight . . ."

Another slap, another, and another. Tears sprang unexpectedly from my eyes.

"Go on, keep singing."

"I want a naked woman tonight . . ."

I could barely move my face; it was buffeted from side to side. I would open my eyes, and they would shut again with the impact of the blows. I didn't know if I was supposed to stop or if I had to obey him . . . but within my pain I had decided something. That was to be my last beating, even if it meant if I had to die.

When he stopped for a moment and ordered me to sing again, I didn't. I looked at him with contempt and said, "Murderer! Go ahead and kill me. You'll get what you deserve in prison!"

Only then did he get up from the chair, seething

with anger. He unbuckled his belt, which had two metal rings, and began to reel off a string of insults. He called me a dog, a waste of space, a good-for-nothing, if that was how I spoke to my father.

He cracked the belt at my body like a whip. It felt like it had a thousand fingers that could hit me all over. I fell to the floor and curled up in a corner by the wall. I was sure he was going to kill me. I was conscious when Glória came to my rescue. Glória, the only sandy-haired one like me. Glória, whom no one touched. She grabbed Papa's hand to stop the blow.

"Papa. Papa. Hit me, for God's sake, but don't hit that child any more."

He threw the belt on the table and ran his hands over his face. He was crying for himself and for me.

"I lost my head. I thought he was taunting me. Giving me cheek."

When Glória picked me up off the ground, I blacked out.

When I came to my senses, I was burning up with fever. Mama and Glória were at my bedside saying sweet things. Lots of people were moving about in the living room. Even Gran had been called. Every movement hurt me all over. Later I learned that they had wanted to call the doctor, but it wouldn't have looked good.

Glória brought me some broth she'd made and tried to feed me a few spoonfuls. I could barely breathe, much less swallow. All I wanted to do was sleep, and each time I woke up, the pain had eased a little. But Mama and Glória continued to watch over me. Mama spent the night with me and didn't get up until just before first light to get ready for work. When she came to say good-bye, I clung to her neck.

"It'll be fine, son. You'll be all good tomorrow."

"Mama . . ."

Quietly I murmured what was, perhaps, the greatest accusation of my life.

"Mama, I shouldn't have been born. I should have been like my balloon . . ."

She sadly stroked my hair.

"Everyone should have been born just as they were. You too. It's just that sometimes, Zezé, you're too naughty."

CHAPTER TEN

A Strange, but Gentle, Request

It took me a week to recover completely. My sadness didn't come from the pain or the blows. At home everyone had started to treat me so well that it was a bit weird. But something was missing. Something important that could make me go back to being myself, perhaps believe in people, believe that they were kind. I was so quiet, so apathetic, almost always sitting beside Pinkie, blankly watching the world go by. I didn't talk to Pinkie or listen to his stories. At the most I'd let my little brother sit with me. I'd play Sugarloaf Mountain with him, which he loved, and let him push the hundred little cable car buttons up and down, all day long. I watched him with great tenderness, because when I was a child, like him, I liked that too.

Glória was worried about my silence. She would set my pile of trading cards and bag of marbles nearby, and sometimes I didn't even move. I didn't feel like going to the cinema or shining shoes. Truth was, I couldn't get over the pain inside me. The pain of a tiny animal that has been brutally beaten and doesn't know why.

Glória asked about my imaginary friends.

"They're not here. They've gone far away."

I meant Fred Thomson and my other friends.

But she didn't know the revolution that was taking place inside me. What I had decided. I was going to change films. I was done with cowboys and Indians and all that. From now on I only wanted to see romantic films, with lots of kissing and hugging, in which everyone liked each other. Since all I was good for was getting beaten up, at least I could see other people liking each other.

The day came when I could go to school. I went, but not to school. I knew Portuga would have been waiting for me in "our" car for a week and had probably given up. Naturally, he would only start waiting again when I told him to. My absence must have worried him a lot. But even if he'd known I was sick, he wouldn't have come looking for me. We had given our word; we'd made a secret pact. No one but God could know about our friendship.

His beautiful car was parked in front of the pastry shop, opposite the train station. The first ray of joy broke through. My heart galloped on ahead, spurred on by my eagerness to see him. I was going to see my one true friend.

But at that moment a beautiful whistle echoed through the station, giving me goose bumps. It was the Mangaratiba. Violent, proud, master of the tracks. It flew past, its cars jiggling in all their splendor. The people at the windows were looking out. Everyone who traveled was happy. When I was little, I liked to watch the Mangaratiba go past while I waved and waved.

I would wave until the train disappeared into the horizon. Now it was Luís who was going through this phase.

I looked around the pastry shop and there he was. At the last table so he could see everyone who came in, but he was looking the other way. He didn't have a jacket on and was wearing his beautiful checkered waistcoat, which showed the white sleeves of his clean shirt.

I suddenly felt so weak I could barely make it over to him. Seu Ladislau tipped him off.

"Look who's here, Portuga."

He slowly turned and his face spread into a smile of happiness. He flung his arms open and gave me a long hug.

"My heart was telling me you'd come today."

Then he gave me a long look.

"So, where've you been all this time?"

"I was very sick."

He pulled out a chair.

"Have a seat."

He snapped his fingers to call over the waiter, who already knew what I liked. But when he set down the soda and pastry in front of me, I didn't even touch them. I rested my head in my arms and stayed like that, feeling frail and sad.

"Don't you want it?"

And because I didn't reply, Portuga lifted up my face. I bit my lips hard and my eyes filled with tears.

"What's all this about, squirt? Tell your old pal here."

"I can't. Not here."

Seu Ladislau was shaking his head as if he didn't understand.

I decided to say something.

"Portuga, is the car still 'our' car?"

"Yes. Do you still doubt it?"

"Could you take me for a drive?"

The request surprised him.

"Sure, if you want to."

He saw that my eyes were even more full of tears, so he took me by the arm, led me to the car, and lifted me into the passenger seat.

He went back to pay the bill, and I heard him talking to Seu Ladislau and the others.

"No one in that boy's family understands him. I've never seen such a sensitive child."

"Tell the truth, Portuga. You really like the little rascal."

"More than you can imagine. He's a wonderful, intelligent little squirt."

He came back to the car and sat down.

"Where do you want to go?"

"I just want to get out of here. We can go to the road to Murundu. It's nearby and won't use up a lot of gas."

He laughed.

"Aren't you too young to understand grown-up problems?"

We were so poor that from an early age we'd learned not to waste money. Everything cost a lot. Gasoline was expensive.

During the short drive he said nothing. He allowed me to collect myself. But when we left everything behind and the landscape became a beautiful blanket of green fields, he stopped the car, looked at me, and smiled, with his kindness that made up for the lack of kindness in the rest of the world.

"Portuga, look at my face. No, not my face, my snout. People at home say I've got a snout because I'm not a person, but an animal, the devil's child."

"I still prefer to look at your face."

"Well, take a good look. See how it's still all swollen from being beaten?"

Portuga's eyes filled with dismay and pity.

"But why did they do that?"

I told him, everything, without exaggerating a single detail. When I finished, his eyes were moist, and for a while he was at a loss for words.

"But it's not right to beat such a young child like that. You're not even six years old. Goodness gracious me!"

"I know why. I'm worthless. I'm so bad that when Christmas comes, the same thing always happens: the devil child is born in my heart instead of the Baby Jesus!"

"Nonsense, you're still a little angel. You might be a little mischievous. . . ."

The idea came back to play on my mind.

"I'm so bad, I shouldn't have been born. I said that to Mama the other day."

For the first time he stammered.

"You shouldn't have said that."

"I asked to speak to you because it's really important. I know it's bad that Papa can't get a job at his age. I know it must hurt a lot. Mama having to leave for work before dawn to help pay the bills. She works the looms at the English Mill. She wears a girdle because she got a hernia loading a box of spools. Lalá's all grown-up, and even though she studied a lot, she has to work at the factory. . . . It's all horrible. But he didn't have to beat me so much. At Christmas, I promised that he could beat me as much as he liked, but this time it was too much."

He was staring at me in disbelief.

"Goodness me! How can such a young child understand and worry about grown-up problems like that? I've never seen anything like it!"

He gulped back a little of his emotion.

"We're friends, aren't we? So let's talk man-to-man. Though, to be honest, sometimes it gives me goose bumps to talk about certain things with you.

First, I don't think you should swear at your sister like that. In fact, you should never swear, you know?"

"But I'm little. It's the only way I can get even."

"Do you know what those words mean?"

I nodded.

"Then you can't and you shouldn't."

We paused.

"Portuga!"

"What?"

"Don't you like me saying swear words?"

"No, I don't."

"OK, then, if I don't die, I promise I won't swear anymore."

"Good. And what's this about dying?"

"I'll tell you when we get there."

We were silent again. The Portuguese was brooding.

"Since you trust me, squirt, I need to know something else. That song, the tango. Did you know what you were singing?"

"I won't lie to you. I wasn't really sure. I learned it because I learn everything. Because it's such a pretty song. I wasn't thinking about what it meant. But he beat me so much, Portuga. But it's OK." I sniffled. "I'm going to kill him."

"What's this, child? You're going to kill your father?"

"Yep. I've already started. Killing him doesn't mean grabbing Buck Jones's revolver and *bang*! That's not it. You can kill someone in your heart. Stop loving them. And one day they die."

"What an imagination you have," he said, unable to hide the emotion that had taken hold of him. "But didn't you say you were going to kill me, too?" he went on.

"That was in the beginning. But then I killed you back to front. I made you die and then you came to life in my heart. You're the only person I like, Portuga. The only friend I have. It's not because you give me trading cards, sodas, sweets, and marbles. . . . I swear it's true."

"But everyone loves you. Your mother, even your father. Your sister Glória, King Luís . . . And have you forgotten your little orange tree? Pinkie . . . What is it you call him?"

"Sweetie."

"So . . ."

"It's different now, Portuga. Truth is, Sweetie is just a simple little orange tree that doesn't even flower. . . . But not you. You're my friend, and that's why I asked to go for a ride in our car, which is soon going to be just yours. I came to say good-bye."

"Good-bye?"

"Yes. You see, I'm good-for-nothing, I'm tired of getting beaten up and having my ears pulled. I'm not going to be another mouth . . ."

I started to feel a painful knot in my throat. I needed courage to say the rest.

"Are you going to run away?"

"No. I spent the whole week thinking about it. Tonight I'm going to throw myself under the Mangaratiba."

He didn't say a word, just hugged me tightly and comforted me as only he knew how.

"No. Don't say that, for the love of God. You have a beautiful life ahead of you. With your mind and your intelligence. It's a sin to say such a thing! I don't want you to think it or say it ever again. What about me? Don't you like me? If you do, and you're not lying, then you shouldn't say things like that." He pulled back from me and looked me in the eye. He wiped away my tears with the back of his hand.

"I'm very fond of you, squirt. Much more than you think. C'mon, give me a smile."

I smiled, somewhat relieved by his confession.

"Soon this will all be forgotten. You'll be master of the streets with your kites, king of the marbles, a cowboy as strong as Buck Jones . . . By the way, I had an idea. Want to know what it is?"

"Yes."

"On Saturday, I'm not going to see my daughter in Encantado. She's gone to spend a few days in Paquetá with her husband. Since the weather's been fine, I was thinking about going fishing over in the Guandu River. I don't have a fishing pal and wondered if you'd like to come."

My eyes lit up.

"Would you take me?"

"Well, if you want. You don't have to come."

My reply was to fling my arms around his neck and hug him, leaning my face against his shaved face. We were laughing and the tragedy had begun to fade.

"I know a beautiful spot. We can take something to eat. What do you like best?"

"You, Portuga."

"I'm talking about salami, eggs, bananas . . ."

"I like everything. At home we learn to like anything and everything."

"Shall we go, then?"

"I won't be able to sleep thinking about it."

But there was a serious problem casting a shadow over our happiness.

"And what will you say about being out of the house the whole day?"

"I'll make something up."

"What if you get caught?"

"No one is allowed to beat me until the end of the month. They promised Glória, and no one messes with Glória. She's the only sandy-haired one like me."

"Really?"

"Really. They can only hit me after one month, when I've recovered."

He started the engine and began to drive back.

"So, do you promise not to talk about it again?"

"About what?"

"The Mangaratiba?"

"It'll take me a while to get around to it. . . ."

"Good to hear."

I later heard, from Seu Ladislau, that despite my promise, Portuga didn't go home until very late that night, after the Mangaratiba had passed.

The drive was beautiful. The road wasn't wide or asphalted, or even paved, but the trees and fields were dazzling. Not to mention the sun and the cheerful bright blue sky. Gran had once said that happiness is a "sun shining in your heart." And that the sun lit up everything with happiness. If it was true, the sun in my heart made everything beautiful.

We talked about certain things again, as the car purred along unhurriedly. It seemed like even the car wanted to listen to our conversation.

"So, when you're with me, you're calm and well behaved. And with your teacher — what's her name again?"

"Dona Cecília Paim. Did you know she has a little white spot in one of her eyes?"

He laughed.

"You said Dona Cecília Paim wouldn't believe the things you do outside school. You're good with your little brother and Glória. So why do you think you change so much?"

"I don't know. All I know is that everything I do leads to trouble. The whole street knows what I've been up to. It's as if the devil whispers things in my ear. Otherwise I wouldn't get up to so much monkey business, as my uncle Edmundo calls it. Do you know what I did once to Uncle Edmundo? I didn't tell you, did I?"

"No."

"Well, it was a good six months ago. He'd gotten a hammock from up north and was really pleased with it. He wouldn't even let us swing in it, the son of a bitch . . ."

"What did you say?"

"Um, the miserable wretch. When he was done with his nap, he'd roll it up and carry it under his arm. As if we were going to steal a piece of it. Well, one day I went to Gran's house, and she didn't see me come in. She must have had her glasses on the end of her nose, reading the classifieds. I went outside. I looked at the guava trees, but I didn't see anything. Then I saw Uncle Edmundo in the hammock, which he'd hung between the fence and the trunk of an orange tree. He was snoring like a pig, his mouth kind of loose and open. His newspaper had fallen on the ground. Then the devil spoke to me, and I saw that there was a box of matches in his pocket. I tore off a bit of paper without making any noise. I piled up the others bits of newspaper and set fire to the wick I'd made. When the flames appeared right beneath his . . ."

I paused and asked earnestly, "Portuga, can I say 'bum'?"

"Well, it's a bit rude and you should try to avoid it."

"So what should we say instead of 'bum'?"

"Posterior."

"What? That's a new one."

"Posterior. POS-TE-RI-OR."

"Well, when it started to burn under his bum's

posterior, I raced out the gate and watched through a hole in the fence to see what would happen. He bellowed. He jumped up and grabbed his hammock. Then Gran came running and gave him a right scolding. 'I'm tired of telling you not to smoke in the hammock!' And when she saw the burning newspaper, she grumbled that she hadn't read that one yet."

The Portuguese chuckled heartily, and I liked seeing him cheerful like that.

"Didn't they catch you?"

"They never found out. I only told Sweetie. If they caught me, they'd have cut my balls off."

"Cut what?"

"I mean, I'd have been in trouble."

He chuckled again and we looked out at the road. Yellow dust rose up everywhere that the car went. But I was mulling something over.

"Portuga, you weren't lying, were you?"

"About what, squirt?"

"Well, I've never heard anyone say: 'He was kicked in the posterior.' Have you?"

He laughed again.

"You're really something. I've never heard it

either. But OK, forget 'posterior' and say 'behind' instead. But let's change the subject or soon I won't know what to say to you. Watch the landscape. You're going to see more and more big trees. We're getting closer to the river."

He turned right and took a shortcut. The car went on and on and then stopped right in an empty field. There was just one big tree with enormous roots.

I clapped my hands with glee.

"How beautiful! What a beautiful place! The next time I see Buck Jones, I'm going to tell him that his prairies and plains don't hold a candle to our place."

He stroked my head.

"This is how I want to see you always. Living out good dreams, not with a head full of crazy ideas."

We got out of the car, and I helped carry the things into the shade of the tree.

"Do you always come here alone, Portuga?"

"Most of the time. See? I have a tree too."

"What's it called, Portuga? If you have a tree this big, you have to give it a name."

He thought for a minute, smiled, and thought some more.

"It's a secret, but I'll tell you. Her name is Queen Carlota."

"And does she talk to you?"

"Not exactly. Because a queen never speaks directly to her subjects. But I always call her 'Your Majesty.'"

"What are 'subjects'?"

"They're the people who do what the queen says."

"Am I your subject?"

He let out such a hearty laugh that it made the grasses stir.

"No, because I'm not a king and I don't give orders. I will always *ask* you to do things."

"But you could be a king. You have everything to be a king. All kings are fat like you. The King of Hearts, the King of Spades, the King of Clubs, and the King of Diamonds. All of the kings in the deck are handsome like you too, Portuga."

"C'mon. Let's get a move on, because all this chatter isn't going to catch us any fish."

He got a fishing rod and a tin can full of worms

and took off his shoes and waistcoat. Without the waistcoat, he looked fatter. He pointed at a place along the river.

"You can play there. It's shallow. But not on the other side, because it's very deep. Now I'm going over there to fish. If you want to stay with me, you can't talk. Otherwise the fish will swim away."

I left him sitting there and went to play. To discover things. How beautiful that piece of river was. I wet my feet and saw a whole bunch of frogs darting here and there in the current. I watched sand, pebbles, and leaves being pulled along by the current. I thought of Glória.

Said the flower to the river
"Leave me, leave me be!
I was born up on the hill . . .
I will die down in the sea."

But the river, quick and cold,
With its mocking song,
Raced over sand and stone,
And swept the flower along.

"Rocking in my cradle,
Rocking in my treetop;
From the sky so blue
Falls the clearest dewdrop!"

Glória was right. The poem was the most beautiful thing in the world. It was a shame I couldn't tell her I'd seen the poem come to life. Not with a flower, but with a bunch of little leaves that had fallen from trees and been carried away to the sea. I wondered if the river, this river, also went to the sea. I could ask the Portuguese. No, it would disturb his fishing.

But he only caught two little fish, which I felt a bit sorry for. The sun was high in the sky. My face was flushed from so much playing and chattering with the world. That was when Portuga came and called me. I skipped over to him like a kid goat.

"Why, you're covered in dirt, squirt."

"I've been playing a lot. I lay on the ground. I splashed in the water. . . ."

"Let's eat. But you can't eat covered in filth like that. Take your clothes off and go have a wash in that shallow spot over there."

I hesitated, unsure whether to obey or not.

"I don't know how to swim."

"But you don't have to. Go ahead—I'll stay nearby."

I stayed where I was. I didn't want him to see the marks, welts, and scars from my beatings.

"Don't tell me you're ashamed to undress in front of me."

"No. It's not that."

I had no choice. I turned around and began to take off my clothes. First my shirt, then my trousers with the cloth belt.

I threw them all on the ground and turned to face him, pleading. He said nothing, but his eyes reflected his indignation and horror.

He just mumbled, "If it hurts, don't get in the water."

"It doesn't hurt anymore."

We ate eggs, bananas, salami, bread, and candied guava, which only I liked. We went to drink water from the river and then returned to the shade of Queen Carlota.

He was about to sit down, but I made a sign for him to stop.

I placed a hand on my chest and addressed the tree.

"Your Majesty, your subject, Sir Manuel Valadares, and the greatest warrior of the Apinajé Nation . . . We are going to sit at Your Majesty's feet."

We laughed and sat.

The Portuguese lay down on the ground, covered a root of the tree with his waistcoat, and said, "Now it's time for a nap."

"But I'm not tired."

"It doesn't matter. I can't let you run loose, mischievous thing that you are."

He placed his hand on my chest and trapped me. We lay there a long while, watching the clouds slip through the branches of the tree. The moment had arrived. If I didn't say it now, I never would.

"Portuga!"

"Yes?"

"Are you asleep?"

"Not yet."

"Is it true what you said to Seu Ladislau at the pastry shop?"

"I've said a lot of things to Seu Ladislau at the pastry shop."

"About me. I heard you. I heard you from the car."

"And what did you hear?"

"That you really like me?"

"Of course I like you. Why do you ask?"

I turned over, without freeing myself from his arms. I stared into his half-closed eyes. His face looked even fatter like that and even more kingly.

"No, but I want to know if you like me lots and lots?"

"Of course, silly."

And he hugged me tighter as proof of what he said.

"I've been doing some serious thinking. You only have that daughter in Encantado, don't you?"

"Yes."

"You live alone in that house with your two bird-cages, don't you?"

"Yes."

"You said you have no grandchildren, right?"

"Yes."

"And you like me, don't you?"

"Yes."

"Then why don't you go to my place and ask Papa to give me to you?"

He was so moved that he sat up and held my face with both hands.

"Would you like to be my son?"

"We don't get to choose our father before we're born. But if I could, I'd choose you."

"Really, squirt?"

"I could even swear it. I'd be one less mouth for them to feed. I promise I'll never say swear words again, not even 'bum.' I'll polish your shoes, look after the birds in the cage. I'll be really well behaved. There won't be a better pupil in the school. I'll be very good."

He didn't even know what to say.

"Everyone will be so happy if I'm given away. It'll be a relief. I have a sister between Glória and

Totoca who was given away to a family in the north. She went to live with a rich cousin to study and have a proper upbringing."

The silence continued and his eyes were full of tears.

"If they don't want to give me away, you can buy me. Papa doesn't have a penny. I'm sure he'll sell me. If he charges a lot, you can buy me in installments, just like people pay Jacob the moneylender . . ."

Because he didn't answer, I resumed my old position and so did he.

"You know, Portuga, if you don't want me, it's OK. I didn't mean to make you cry. . . ."

He stroked my hair for a long time.

"That's not it, son. That's not it. We can't solve our problems just like that, with a snap of the fingers. But I have a suggestion. Much as I'd like to, I can't take you away from your parents or your home. It isn't right. But from now on, even though I already thought of you as a son, I'm going to treat you as if you really were my own."

I sat up, elated.

"Really, Portuga?"

"I could even swear it, as you always say."

I did something that I rarely did or wanted to do with the members of my family. I kissed him on his fat, kind face.

CHAPTER ELEVEN

Little by Little, Tenderness Is Born

"'None of them could speak, and you couldn't go horseback riding on them either, Portuga?'

"'None of them.'

"'But you weren't a child then?'

"'I was. But not all children are lucky enough to understand trees like you do. And it isn't every tree that likes to talk.'

"He gave an affectionate laugh and went on.

"'They weren't exactly trees, but trellised vines,

and before you ask: trellised vines are what grapes grow on. They're just thick vines. It was pretty to see the harvests and the grape stomping.'

"He explained what that was. He seemed to know a lot. As much as Uncle Edmundo.

"'Tell me more.'

"'You're enjoying it?'

"'Very much. I wish I could talk with you non-stop for 852 miles.'

"'What about the gasoline for all that?'

"'It's make-believe gasoline.'

"Then he told me about the grass that turns into hay in winter and about cheese-making. He says 'cheese' differently from us. He changes the music of the words a lot, but I think they sound even more musical.

"He stopped talking and gave a long sigh.

"'I'd like to go back there very soon. Perhaps to spend my twilight years in a peaceful, enchanted place. Folhadela, near Monreal, in my beautiful Trás-os-Montes.'

"It was only then that I really noticed that Portuga was older than Papa, although his plump face was always shiny, with fewer wrinkles. A strange feeling ran through me.

"'Are you serious?'

"Only then did he notice my disappointment.

"'Don't worry, silly — it's a long way off. It might never even happen.'

"'What about me? It took so long for you to be like this, the way I like you.'

"My eyes filled with cowardly tears.

"'But surely I'm allowed to dream too.'

"'It's just that you didn't put me in your dream.'

"He smiled dotingly.

"'I put you in all my dreams, Portuga. When I head out over the green prairies with Tom Mix and Fred Thomson, I've already hired a stagecoach for you to travel in so you don't get tired. You're everywhere I go. Sometimes at school I look up and imagine you've come to wave at me from the door.'

"'Goodness me! I've never seen a soul as starved for affection as you. But you shouldn't be so attached to me, you know?'"

I was telling all this to Pinkie. Pinkie liked to talk more than I did.

"But the truth is, after he became my father, Sweetie, he's been all doting. He thinks everything I do is cute. But a different cute. He's not like other people who say, 'That boy'll go far. He'll go far, but he'll never leave Bangu.'"

I gave Pinkie a tender look. Now that I'd discovered what tenderness was, I lavished it on everything that I liked.

"You see, Pinkie, I want to have twelve children and then twelve more. Do you understand? The first lot will all be children and no one will ever lay a finger on them. The other twelve will grow into men. And I'll go and ask each of them, 'What do you most want to be, son? A woodcutter? Right, then. Here's an ax and a checkered shirt. You want to be a lion tamer? Well, here's a whip and a uniform.'"

"What about at Christmas? What are you going to do with so many children?"

Pinkie was really something! Interrupting at a time like that.

"At Christmas I'm going to have lots of money. I'll buy a truckload of chestnuts and hazelnuts. Walnuts, figs, and raisins. So many toys that they'll give or lend them to our poor neighbors. . . . And I'm going to have lots of money, because from now on I want to be rich, really rich, and I'm going to win the lottery too. . . ."

I looked at Pinkie defiantly, to show that I wasn't happy about his interruption.

"Let me finish telling you the rest 'cause there are lots of children to go. 'So, son, you want to be a cowboy? Here's your saddle and lasso. You want to drive the Mangaratiba? Here's your cap and whistle. . . .'"

"Why a whistle, Zezé? You talk to yourself so much, you'll end up going crazy."

Totoca had come over to sit by me. With a friendly smile, he studied my orange tree, covered in string and beer caps. He wanted something.

"Zezé, do you want to lend me four tostões?"

"No."

"But you have it, don't you?"

"Yep."

"And you don't want to lend it to me even though you don't know what it's for?"

"I'm going to become very rich so I can travel to Trás-os-Montes."

"What's all this about?"

"Not telling."

"Well, keep it to yourself, then."

"I will, but I'm not lending you four tostões."

"You're good at marbles. You're a good shot. Tomorrow you'll play and win more marbles to sell. You'll get your four tostões back in no time."

"It doesn't matter. I won't lend it to you, and don't come here to pick a fight with me, 'cause I'm behaving myself and not up to any mischief."

"I'm not here to pick a fight. It's just that you're my favorite brother, and now all of a sudden you're becoming a heartless monster."

"I'm not becoming a heartless monster. I'm a heartless troglodyte."

"What's that?"

"Troglodyte. Uncle Edmundo showed me a picture in a magazine. They were big hairy monkeys with clubs. Troglodytes were people at the beginning of the world who lived in the caves of Nean . . .

Ne-an . . . I don't know. I can't remember the name because it was foreign and too difficult."

"Uncle Edmundo shouldn't fill your head with so many ideas. But will you lend it to me?"

"I don't even know if I have it. . . ."

"C'mon, Zezé, how many times have we gone out to shine shoes and you didn't make a thing and I shared what I made with you? How many times have I carried your box when you were tired . . . ?"

It was true. Totoca was rarely mean to me. I knew I'd end up lending it to him.

"If you lend it to me, I'll tell you two really good things."

I was silent.

"And I'll say that your sweet orange tree is much more beautiful than my tamarind tree."

"Really?"

"That's what I said."

I put my hand in my pocket and shook my coins.

"What else?"

"You know, Zezé, we're not going to be poor anymore. Papa got a job as a manager at Santo Aleixo

Factory. We're going to be rich again. . . . What's wrong? Aren't you happy?"

"Yes, I'm happy for Papa. But I don't want to leave Bangu. I'll go live with Gran. I'm only leaving here to go to Trás-os-Montes. . . ."

"Right. You'd rather stay with Gran and take laxatives once a month than go with us?"

"Yep. And you'll never know why. . . . What's the other thing?"

"I can't tell you here. There's 'someone' who can't hear it."

We walked over to the outhouse. Even so, he spoke in a low voice.

"I need to warn you, Zezé. So you can get used to the idea. City Hall is planning to make the streets wider. They're going to fill in all the ditches and take space from all the backyards."

"So what?"

"You're such a bright spark and you didn't get it? When they widen the streets, they're going to tear all that down."

He pointed at the place where my sweet orange

tree stood. I puckered up to cry.

"You're lying, aren't you, Totoca?"

"You don't need to make that face. It's still a long way off."

My fingers were nervously counting the coins in my pocket.

"It's a lie, isn't it, Totoca?"

"No. It's the honest-to-God truth. But are you a big boy or not?"

"I am."

The tears streamed down my face anyway. I hugged him around the waist, begging.

"You're with me, aren't you, Totoca? I'm going to round up a lot of people to make war. No one's chopping down my little orange tree."

"OK, fine. We won't let them. Now will you lend me the money?"

"What's it for?"

"Since you were banned from the Cinema Bangu, they started showing a Tarzan film. I'll tell you all about it when I've seen it."

I found five tostões in my pocket and handed

him the money while I dried my eyes with the bottom of my shirt.

"Keep the change. You can buy some sweets."

I went back to my orange tree, but I didn't feel like talking. I just thought about the Tarzan film. I'd seen it the day before.

"Do you want to go?" Portuga had asked when I told him about it.

"I'd love to, but I'm not allowed in the Cinema Bangu."

I reminded him why. He laughed.

"Is that head of yours making things up?"

"I swear, Portuga. But I think if a grown-up went with me, no one would say anything."

"And if this grown-up were me . . . Is that what you want?"

My face lit up with happiness.

"But I have to work, son."

"There's never anyone there at this time. Instead of chatting or napping in the car, you could see Tarzan fighting leopards, alligators, and gorillas. Do you know who plays Tarzan? Frank Merrill."

But he still wasn't sure.

"You little rascal. You've a ruse for everything."

"It's only two hours. You're already very rich, Portuga."

"Let's go, then. But let's walk there. I'm going to leave my car parked right here."

And we went. But the girl at the ticket counter said she had strict orders not to let me in for one year.

"I'll be responsible for him. That was before. He knows how to behave now."

The ticket girl looked at me, and I smiled at her. I planted a kiss on the tips of my fingers and blew it to her.

"Look here, Zezé. If you get up to anything, I'll lose my job."

I'd been keeping our trip to the cinema a secret from Pinkie, but I could never keep anything from him for long.

CHAPTER TWELVE

The Mangaratiba

When Dona Cecília Paim asked if anyone wanted to come up to the blackboard to write a sentence they had made up themselves, no one dared. But I thought of something and put my hand up.

"Want to come up here, Zezé?"

As I stood and walked to the blackboard, I was proud to hear her say, "See? The youngest member of class."

I couldn't even reach halfway up the blackboard. I took the chalk and wrote in my best handwriting:

There are only a few days left until the holidays.

I looked at Dona Cecília Paim to see if I'd made a mistake. She smiled happily and on her desk was the empty glass. Empty, but with an imaginary rose in it, as she had said.

I returned to my desk, happy with my sentence. Happy because, come the holidays, I was going to see Portuga a lot.

Then others put up their hands, wanting to write sentences. But I was the hero.

Someone asked if they could come in. They were running late. It was Jerônimo. He came bumbling in and sat directly behind me. He plonked his books down noisily and said something to the person next to him. I didn't pay much attention. I wanted to study to be wise. But one word in the whispered conversation caught my attention. They were talking about the Mangaratiba.

"It hit the car?"

"Manuel Valadares's car. That beautiful one."

I swung around in shock.

"What did you say?"

"I said the Mangaratiba hit the Portuguese's car

·234·

on the crossing at Rua da Chita. That's why I'm late. The train crushed the car. There's a huge crowd there. They even called the Realengo Fire Brigade."

I broke into a cold sweat and it felt like everything was about to go black. Jerônimo continued answering his neighbor's questions.

"I don't know if he's dead. They wouldn't let children anywhere near it."

Without realizing it, I stood up. I felt a terrible need to throw up, and my body was covered in cold sweat. I left my desk and headed for the door. I barely even registered the face of Dona Cecília Paim, who had come to intercept me. Perhaps she'd seen the color drain from my face.

"What's wrong, Zezé?"

But I couldn't answer. Tears were welling in my eyes. Then something snapped and I bolted, without even thinking about the headmistress's office. I reached the street and forgot about the highway, about everything. I just wanted to run and run until I got there. My heart hurt more than my stomach, and I ran the length of Rua das Casinhas without stopping. I got to the pastry shop and glanced about at the cars to see if Jerônimo was lying. But our car wasn't there. I let out a cry and started running again. I was caught by Seu Ladislau's strong arms.

"Where're you going, Zezé?"

My face was wet with tears.

"There."

"You don't have to."

I struggled like crazy but couldn't free myself.

"Calm down, son. I won't let you go."

"So the Mangaratiba *did* kill him. . . ."

"No. The ambulance has come already. It just wrecked the car."

"You're lying, Seu Ladislau."

"Why would I lie? Didn't I tell you the train hit the car? So, when he's allowed to have visitors at the hospital, I'll take you, I promise. Now, let's go have a soda."

He took a handkerchief and wiped away my sweat.

"I'm going to be a little sick."

I leaned against the wall, and he held my head.

"Feeling better, Zezé?"

I nodded.

"I'll take you home, OK?"

I shook my head and began to walk slowly away, in a daze. I knew the truth. The Mangaratiba was merciless. It was the strongest train there was. I threw up a few more times, and I could see that no one paid the slightest attention. I had no one left in the world. I didn't go back to school and just followed my heart. I sniffed from time to time and dried my face on my school uniform. I'd never see my Portuga again. Never again. He was gone. I walked and walked. I stopped at the road where he'd let me call him Portuga and let me piggyback on his car. I sat at the base of a tree trunk and curled up, face on my knees.

Suddenly I blurted out, "You're mean, Baby Jesus. I thought you were going to be good to me this time, and you go and do this? Why don't you like me as much as the other boys? I've been good. I haven't fought, I've done my homework, I've stopped swearing. I even stopped saying 'bum.' Why have you done this to me, Baby Jesus? They're going to cut down my orange tree, and I didn't even get upset about it. I only cried a little bit. . . . But now . . . now . . ."

My outburst surprised me. A new flood of tears.

"I want my Portuga back, Baby Jesus. You have to give me my Portuga back."

Then a very soft, very sweet voice spoke to my heart. It must have been the friendly voice of the tree I was sitting under.

"Don't cry, child. He's in heaven."

When it was almost dark, Totoca found me sitting on Dona Helena Villas-Boas's doorstep, drained of all strength, unable to throw up or cry anymore.

He spoke to me, but all I could do was moan.

"What's wrong, Zezé? Talk to me."

I just kept moaning in a low voice. Totoca put his hand on my forehead.

"You're burning up with fever. What's going on, Zezé? Come with me; let's go home. I'll help you; we'll go slow."

I managed to speak between moans.

"Forget it, Totoca. I'm not going back to that house."

"Yes, you are. It's our house."

"There's nothing left for me there. It's all over."

He tried to help me up, but he saw that I didn't have the strength.

He wrapped my arms around his neck and carried me in his arms. When we got home, he laid me down on the bed.

"Jandira! Glória! Where is everyone?"

He went to find Jandira, who was chatting with Alaíde at her house.

"Jandira, Zezé's really sick."

She came, grumbling.

"He must be up to something. A few good smacks with a sandal . . ."

But Totoca had walked nervously into the bedroom.

"No, Jandira. This time he's really sick and he's going to die."

For three days and three nights, I didn't want a thing. I was burning up with fever and threw up every time they tried to give me something to eat or drink. I was wasting away. I just lay there motionless, staring at the wall for hours on end.

I heard people around me talking. I understood everything they said, but I didn't want to answer. I didn't want to talk. All I could think about was going to heaven.

Glória changed rooms and spent the nights by my side. She wouldn't let anyone turn off the light. Everyone treated me with kid gloves. Even Gran came to spend a few days with us.

Totoca spent hours and hours with me, eyes bulging, talking from time to time.

"It's not true, Zezé. Honestly. It was all a lie. They're not going to widen the streets or anything. . . ."

The house was cloaked in silence as if death walked in silk slippers. No one made any noise. They all spoke quietly. Mama spent almost the entire night with me. But I couldn't forget him. His laughter. His way of talking. Even the crickets outside imitated the *kechah*, *kechah* of him shaving. I couldn't stop thinking about him. Now I really knew what pain was. Pain wasn't being beaten unconscious. It wasn't cutting my foot on a shard of glass and getting stitches at the pharmacy. Pain was this: my whole heart ached, and I had to carry it to the grave. I couldn't tell anyone my secret. Pain sapped the strength from my arms, my head; I didn't even want to turn my head on the pillow.

And it only got worse. I was skin and bones. They called the doctor. Dr. Faulhaber came and examined me. It didn't take him long to figure it out.

"It's shock. He's deeply traumatized. He'll only survive if he is able to get over it."

Glória took the doctor outside and told him.

"He *has* had a shock, sir. He's been like this ever since he heard they're planning to cut down his orange tree."

"Then you need to convince him that it isn't true."

"We've tried everything, but he won't believe us. To him, the tree is a person. He's an odd boy. Very sensitive and precocious."

I overheard it all, but I still didn't want to live. I wanted to go to heaven, and no one went there alive.

They bought medicine, but I kept on throwing up.

That was when something beautiful happened.

Everyone in the street started coming to visit me. They forgot that I was the devil incarnate. Seu Misery and Hunger came and brought me a marshmallow. Eugênia brought me eggs and prayed over my belly so I would stop throwing up.

"Seu Paulo's son is dying."

They said nice things to me.

"You need to get better, Zezé. The street's so sad without you and your mischief."

Dona Cecília Paim came to see me, with my satchel and a flower. It just made me start crying all over again.

She said I'd left the classroom and that was the last she'd heard of me.

But it was really sad when Seu Ariovaldo came to see me. I recognized his voice and pretended to be asleep.

"You can wait outside until he wakes up."

He sat down and said to Glória, "Listen, ma'am, I went along asking everyone where he lived until I found the house."

He sniffed loudly.

"My little saint can't die. Don't let him, ma'am.

It was you he brought my brochures to, wasn't it?"

Glória was barely able to reply.

"Don't let the li'l critter die, ma'am. If anything happens to him, I'll never come to this godforsaken part of town again."

When he came into the room, he sat next to the bed and pressed my hand to his face.

"Look here, Zezé. You need to get well and come sing again. I've barely sold a thing. Everyone says, 'Hey, Ariovaldo, where's your little canary?' Promise you're going to get well. Promise?"

My eyes filled with tears, and Glória, seeing that I was upset again, led Seu Ariovaldo away.

I started to improve. I was able to swallow things and keep them down. But whenever I remembered, the fever would come back higher than ever, along with the throwing up. Sometimes I saw the Mangaratiba hurtling along and crushing him. I couldn't help it. I prayed to Baby Jesus, if he cared about me at all, that he hadn't felt anything.

Glória would come and stroke my head.

"Don't cry, shrimp. It'll all pass. If you want, my

mango tree is all yours. No one's going to do anything to it."

But what was I going to do with a toothless old mango tree that didn't even bear fruit anymore? Even my orange tree would soon lose its charm and become a tree like any other. . . . That's if they gave the poor thing a chance.

How easy it was for some to die. A cruel train just had to come along and that was it. And how hard it was for me to get to heaven. Everyone was holding on to my legs so I couldn't go.

Glória's kindness and devotion managed to get me talking a little. Papa even stopped going out at night. Totoca lost so much weight out of remorse that Jandira gave him a scolding.

"Isn't one sickly person enough, Totoca?"

"You're not in my shoes to feel what I'm feeling. I was the one who told him. I can still feel it in my stomach, even when I'm sleeping, his face, crying and crying."

"Now, don't you go crying too. You're a big boy, and he's going to pull through. Now, chin up and go buy me a can of condensed milk at the Misery and Hunger."

"Then give me the money 'cause he won't keep a tab for Papa anymore."

My weakness made me constantly sleepy. I no longer knew when it was day or night. The fever would ease a little, and my tremors and agitation would let up. I would open my eyes and, in the semi-darkness, there would be Glória, who never left my side. She had brought the rocking chair into the room and often fell asleep in it, she was so tired.

"Gló, is it afternoon already?"

"Almost, my love."

"Do you want to open the window?"

"Won't it make your head hurt?"

"I don't think so."

The light came in, and I could see a sliver of beautiful sky. I took one look at it and started to cry again.

"What's the matter, Zezé? The Baby Jesus made such a beautiful blue sky for you. He told me so today. . . ."

Gloria didn't know that the sky reminded me of heaven.

She leaned over, took my hands in hers, and tried to cheer me up. Her face was tired and thin.

"Look, Zezé, soon you'll be better. Flying kites, winning a heap of marbles, climbing trees, riding Pinkie. I want to see you back to your old self, singing songs, bringing me lyrics. So many beautiful things. See how sad the street is lately? Everyone misses the life and cheer you bring to it. But you have to help. Live, live, and live."

"But I don't want to anymore, Gló. If I get better, I'll be bad again. You don't understand. I don't have anyone to be good for anymore."

"Well, you don't need to be *that* good. Be a boy. Be the child you always were."

"What for, Gló? So everyone can hit me again? So everyone can treat me badly?"

She took my face between her fingers and said resolutely, "Look, shrimp. I promise you one thing. When you get better, no one, but no one, not even God, is going to lay a finger on you. They'd have to step over my cold cadaver first! Do you believe me?"

I nodded.

"What's a cadaver?"

For the first time, Glória's face lit up with happiness. She laughed, because she knew that if I was interested in difficult words, I had regained my will to live.

"A cadaver's a dead body, a corpse. But maybe we should change the subject now."

I thought it was a good idea, too, but I couldn't help but think that *he* had been a cadaver for several days now. Glória kept talking, promising things, but now I was thinking about Portuga's two little birds, the blue one and the canary. What would become of them? They might have died of sadness like Orlando-Hair-on-Fire's finch. Maybe someone had opened the cage doors and set them free. But that would have meant certain death. They didn't know how to fly anymore. They would sit in the orange trees until the children hit them with their slingshots. When Zico couldn't afford to keep the tanager aviary going, he had opened the doors and that's what happened. Not one escaped.

Things began to return to normal in the house.

There was noise everywhere. Mama went back to work. The rocking chair went back to the sitting room, where it had always lived. Only Glória stayed put. She wasn't going to budge until she saw me standing again.

"Have this soup, shrimp. Jandira killed the black chicken just to make this soup for you. See how nice it smells."

And she would blow on the spoon.

If you like, dunk your bread in the coffee like this. But don't slurp when you take a sip. It's bad manners.

"Hey, what's going on, shrimp? Don't tell me you're going to cry because the black chicken is dead. She was old. So old she didn't lay eggs anymore."

So you managed to find out where I live.

"I know she was the black panther at the zoo, but we'll buy another black panther, much wilder than her."

So, where've you been all this time?

"Not now, Gló. If I eat it, I'll start throwing up."

"If I give it to you later, will you have it?"

And before I could stop myself, I blurted out, "I promise to be good, I won't fight, I won't use swear

·248·

words, not even 'bum.' But I always want to be with you."

They gave me worried looks, thinking I was talking to Pinkie again.

In the beginning it was just a rustling at the window, but after that it turned into knocking. A gentle voice came from outside.

"Zezé!"

I got up and leaned my head against the shutter.

"Who is it?"

"It's me. Open up."

I unlatched it without making any noise so as not to wake Glória. Standing there in the darkness was Pinkie, all shiny and festooned with gold, like a miracle.

"May I come in?"

"I guess so. But don't make any noise or she'll wake up."

"I promise not to wake her."

He jumped into the room, and I went back to bed.

"Look who I brought to see you. He insisted on coming too."

He held out his arm, and I saw a kind of silver bird.

"I can't see properly, Pinkie."

"Pay attention because you're going to get a surprise. I dressed him up with silver feathers. Isn't he beautiful?"

"Luciano! How fine you look. You should stay like that forever. I thought you were a falcon from *The Tale of Caliph Stork*."

I stroked his head, overcome with emotion, and felt for the first time that it was soft and that even bats liked tenderness.

"You missed something. Take a good look."

Pinkie turned around to show himself off.

"I'm wearing Tom Mix's spurs. Ken Maynard's hat. Fred Thomson's pistols. Richard Talmadge's belt and boots. And to top it off, Seu Ariovaldo lent me that checkered shirt you like so much."

"I've never seen anything more beautiful, Pinkie. How did you get it all?"

"When they heard you weren't well, they lent it to me."

"It's a shame you can't dress like that all the time."

I studied Pinkie, worried that he might know what awaited him. But I didn't say anything.

He sat on the edge of the bed, and his eyes were all sweetness and concern. He leaned in close.

"What's wrong, Sweetie?" he said.

"But you're Sweetie, Pinkie."

"Well, then you're Sweetie Junior. Can't I be a really good friend to you, as you are to me?"

"Don't say that. The doctor told me not to cry."

"I don't want that either. I came because I really miss you, and I want to see you well and happy again. Everything in life passes. And to prove it, I've come to take you for a ride. Let's go?"

"I'm very weak."

"A little fresh air will cure you. I'll help you jump out the window."

And we left.

"Where are we going?"

"Let's go for a walk on the water pipes."

"But I don't want to go down Rua Barão de

Capanema. I'm never going there again."

"Let's take Rua dos Açudes right to the end."

Pinkie had transformed into a flying horse. Luciano was perched happily on my shoulder.

When we got there, Pinkie gave me his hand to help me balance on the thick pipes. It was nice when there was a hole and the water squirted up like a little fountain, wetting us and tickling the soles of my feet. I felt a little dizzy, but the joy that Pinkie was giving me made me feel as if I was better already. At least my heart was lighter.

Suddenly, I heard a whistle in the distance.

"Did you hear that, Pinkie?"

"It's a train whistle, far away."

But a strange noise grew closer and closer, and new whistles pierced the silence. The horror hit me all at once.

"It's the train, Pinkie. The Mangaratiba. The murderer!"

And the sound of the wheels on the tracks grew, frighteningly.

"Climb up here, Pinkie. Quickly, Pinkie."

Pinkie couldn't keep his balance on the pipe because of the shiny spurs.

"C'mon, Pinkie, give me your hand. It wants to kill you. It wants to kill you. It wants to crush you. It wants to chop you up."

Pinkie had barely climbed onto the pipe when the wicked train charged past, whistling and blowing out steam.

"Murderer! Murderer!"

But the train continued speeding over the tracks. Its voice came to us between fits of laughter.

"It wasn't my fault. . . . It wasn't my fault. . . . It wasn't my fault. . . . It wasn't my fault. . . ."

All the lights in the house came on, and my room was invaded by sleepy-eyed faces.

"It was a nightmare."

Mama took me in her arms, trying to quell my sobs against her chest.

"It was just a dream, son. . . . A bad dream."

I began to throw up again while Glória told Lalá what had happened.

"I woke up to him shouting 'Murderer.' He was

talking about killing, crushing, chopping . . . My God, when is all this going to end?"

But a few days later, it ended. I was condemned to go on living and living. One morning, Glória came in, radiant. I was sitting up in bed, feeling sad about life.

"Look, Zezé."

In her hands was a tiny white flower.

"It's Pinkie's first blossom. Soon he'll be a grown-up tree and bear fruit."

I sat there stroking the little white flower. I wouldn't cry over anything anymore. Although Pinkie was trying to say good-bye to me with that flower, he had already left the world of my dreams for the world of my reality and pain.

"Now let's have some porridge and walk around the house a little like you did yesterday. Come soon, OK?"

That was when King Luís climbed onto my bed. He was allowed near me now. At first they hadn't wanted him to get upset.

"Zezé!"

"What, my little king?"

He was the only true king. The others — the King of Diamonds, the King of Hearts, the King of Clubs, and the King of Spades — were just figures soiled by the fingers that played them. But he wouldn't live to sit on a throne.

"Zezé, I love you."

"I love you too, little brother."

"Do you want to play with me today?"

"Yes, I'll play with you today. What do you want to do?"

"I want to go to the zoo, and then to Europe. Then I want to go to the Amazon jungle and play with Pinkie."

"If I don't get too tired, we can do it all."

After breakfast, as Glória looked on happily, we went down to the back of the yard holding hands. Glória leaned in the doorway, relieved. Before we reached the chicken coop, I turned and waved at her. Her eyes glowed with happiness. And I, with my strange precociousness, sensed what she was feeling in her heart: "He's gone back to his dream world, thank God!"

"Zezé?"

"Yes?"

"Where's the black panther?"

It was hard to go back to playing the same old games now that I didn't believe in such things anymore. I felt like saying, "There never was a black panther, silly. It was just an old black hen, which I ate in a soup."

But I said, "There are only two lions left, Luís. The black panther went on a vacation to the Amazon jungle."

Best to preserve his illusions as much as possible. When I was little, I believed those things too.

The little king opened his eyes wide.

"In that jungle, over there?'

"Don't be afraid. She went so far that she'll never be able to find her way back."

I smiled bitterly. The Amazon jungle was just half a dozen thorny and hostile orange trees.

"You know, Luís, I'm feeling weak. I need to go back in. We'll play more tomorrow. Cable cars and whatever else you want."

He nodded and slowly followed me back to the

house. He was still too young to know the truth. I didn't want to go anywhere near the ditch or the Amazon River. I didn't want to see Pinkie with his spell broken. Luís didn't know that the tiny white flower had been our good-bye.

CHAPTER THIRTEEN

Many Are the Old Trees

The news was confirmed before nightfall. Apparently peace was to reign once again over our home and family.

Papa took me by the hand and sat me on his lap in front of everyone. He rocked the chair slowly so I wouldn't get dizzy.

"It's all over, son. Everything. One day you'll be a father and you'll see how difficult certain moments in a man's life are. Nothing seems to go right, and you feel a desperation that's never ending. But not anymore. I've been made a manager at the Santo Aleixo Factory. Your shoes will never be empty at Christmas again."

He paused. He would never forget *that* Christmas for the rest of his life.

"We're going to travel a lot. Mama won't need to work anymore, or your sisters. Do you still have the medallion with the Indian on it?"

I rummaged in my pocket and found it.

"Well, I'm going to buy a new watch and put the medallion on it. One day it will be yours."

Portuga, do you know what carborundum is?

Papa talked and talked.

His stubble rubbing against my face bothered me. The smell coming from his well-worn shirt gave me goose bumps. I slipped off his knee and went to the kitchen door. I sat on the steps and gazed at the backyard as the light faded. My heart protested without anger. "Who is this man who puts me on his knee? He isn't my father. My father is dead. The Mangaratiba killed him."

Papa had followed me and saw that my eyes were full of tears again.

He practically knelt to speak to me.

"Don't cry, son. We're going to have a big house. A real river runs right behind it. There are big trees, lots of them, and they'll all be yours. You can make swings and hang them there."

He didn't understand. He didn't understand. No tree could ever be as beautiful as Queen Carlota.

"You'll have first pick of the trees."

I looked at his feet, his toes poking out of his sandals. He was an old tree with dark roots. He was a tree-father. But a tree I barely knew.

"That's not all. They're not going to cut down your orange tree so soon. And when they do, you'll be far away and won't even feel it."

I clung to his knees, sobbing.

"It's no use, Papa. It's no use. . . ."

And looking at his face, which was also streaked with tears, I mumbled like a dead man, "It's gone, Papa. My sweet orange tree was cut down over a week ago."

CHAPTER FOURTEEN

Final Confession

The years have passed, my dear Manuel Valadares. I am forty-eight years old now, and sometimes I miss you so much I feel like I am still a child. I imagine that at any moment you'll appear with trading cards and marbles. It was you who taught me what tenderness is, my dear Portuga. Today I am the one who tries to hand out marbles and trading cards, because life without tenderness isn't very special. Sometimes I am happy in my tenderness, and sometimes I think I'm kidding myself, which is more common.

Back then, back in our time, I didn't know that many years earlier, an idiot prince had knelt before an altar and asked the saints, his eyes full of tears:

> "Why do they tell little children
> so much so young?"

The truth, my dear Portuga, is that they told me things way too soon.

Farewell!

Ubatuba, 1967

A FEW WORDS FROM THE TRANSLATOR

Dear reader,

Originally published in 1968, *My Sweet Orange Tree* is a Brazilian classic and one of the country's best-selling novels of all time, adopted by schools and adapted for cinema, television, and the stage. It has also been translated into nineteen languages and continues to be very popular in countries all over the world today. It is set in Bangu, an outlying neighborhood of Rio de Janeiro, where the author, José Mauro de Vasconcelos, grew up. The story is, to the best of my knowledge, based on his own life and, although narrated by a middle-aged man, reflects the point of view of a five-year-old child. Despite the book's apparent simplicity, the translation actually took quite a lot of detective work, due to the fact that it takes place in the 1920s and many aspects of life in Brazil have long since changed. Also, sadly, the author is no longer around to consult.

For example, I spent a long time researching something called a mão de couro (literally "leather hand"), which is used to mete out corporal punishment. I suspected it was some kind of whip but couldn't find it in any dictionary or encyclopedia. An Internet search turned up only a few obscure links, and no one in the translation forums I consulted had ever heard of it. As a last resort, I turned to a forum of Brazilian writers and was relieved when a woman wrote to me confirming that it was indeed an old-fashioned whipping device, one of which she had seen hanging behind her grandfather's kitchen door when she was a girl. Somewhat hand-like in appearance, it had five long leather "fingers" designed to multiply the effects of the lashing. I have called it a "leather strap" in the translation, as I feel that "leather hand" is too puzzling and could give rise to other interpretations.

Equally as baffling was a reference to caveirinhas ("little skulls") tangled in wires, which, from the context, I take to be kite frames caught in overhead electric wires, whose tissue-paper "bodies" have been stripped away from their flimsy wooden structures by the wind. From the casual way José Mauro de Vasconcelos uses the word, I suspect that caveirinha was the slang term for this in 1920s Bangu, though I will probably never know for sure. I have translated it as "kite skeletons," for the sake of comprehension, as I don't think it was meant to be cryptic.

There is also a mysterious quote and reference to an "idiot prince" at the end of the book, which I believe to be a reference to Dostoyevsky's Prince Myshkin in *The Idiot,* though, again, without the author around to confirm it, I can't be one hundred percent sure.

I have standardized all references to money, as Brazil has changed currency no fewer than eight times since this story took place, and the relationship between the different coins in circulation back then would probably be lost on anyone but a numismatist. The currency in the 1920s was, like today, known as the real (plural réis), and the tostão (plural tostões), worth about a penny, is the coin most used in this book. For ease of understanding, I have converted everything into tostões.

Brazilians are consummate nicknamers. In addition to deftly whittling names down to single syllables (I have been called both "Li" and "A"), they also love to bestow made-up nicknames—with touches of black humor—on people and places that have nothing to do with their actual names. The Misery and Hunger, a corner-bar-and-grocery-store, is one such example. The character Orlando-Hair-on-Fire is another.

After many years of translating Brazilian literature and discussing it with both authors and editors, I have come to the conclusion that there are fundamental differences between the ways Anglophones and Brazilians tell stories. Many writers, and it is certainly the case with José Mauro de Vasconcelos, don't present things in quite the same way that we do. Characters, objects, and concepts can appear rather suddenly, as they become relevant, without any additional information to explain them. Details about who or what they are must be gathered from multiple sites across the narrative. Other characters make one-off cameo appearances and disappear for good (like Orlando-Hair-on-Fire, mentioned above). Brazilian readers, who are more accustomed to this phenomenon, tend to take it in stride, whereas it can leave English-language readers wondering if they've missed something. So if you find yourself perplexed by a character you haven't met before, consider this your introduction and keep an eye out for future appearances. I find this a charming aspect of Brazilian storytelling, one that reflects the spontaneity of the people and the culture, and am reluctant to "iron it out" in the translation.

Luckily most things aren't too inscrutable, and I prefer to let readers parse them from the context, just as, when we travel, we come across unfamiliar objects and customs that, though odd, are perfectly decipherable.

Alison Entrekin